TROUBLE WITH THE HOTSHOT BOSS

TROUBLE WITH THE HOTSHOT BOSS

USA TODAY BESTSELLING AUTHOR

HOLLY RENEE

For Kya Milicic—

Your support means everything to me.
This one's for you.

CONTENT WARNING

This book contains depictions of sexually explicit scenes. It contains mature language, themes, and content that may not be suitable for all readers. Reader discretion is advised.

PROLOGUE
SOPHIE

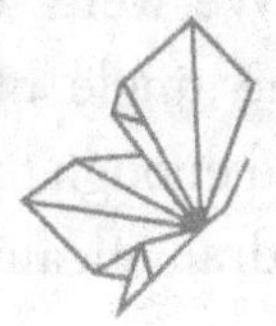

Five Years Earlier

I was a little bit tipsy, but I knew with one hundred percent certainty that Jase Hale was the hottest boy I had ever seen.

I had known that fact since I first laid eyes on him at ten years old. Not that I understood what hot was at that age, but I knew there was a reason I couldn't stop smiling when I was around him.

It had nothing to do with the fact that he and my brother loved spending time with me. It was the opposite actually.

But I didn't care.

It was my eighteenth birthday, and he was here.

They all were. My brother, Tucker, and all of his best friends.

They were a bit shocked by all the alcohol I had managed to commandeer without their help, but I wasn't the same little girl they had all left behind once they graduated high school.

Jase knew it too. He didn't check my ass out in my skin-tight jeans like I was his best friend's little sister.

And he had been watching me all night.

"You want another drink?" I leaned against the wall beside him and turned my head to take him in fully.

"I'm good." He shook the cup in his hand, but he turned his head to look at me. We were so close to each other. I could practically feel the tingle of the mint gum in his mouth. "I think you've had enough too."

I rolled my eyes dramatically. "I've barely drunk anything."

"Happy birthday, Soph." Elliott, a boy from my grade, walked by, and I smiled before turning back to Jase.

He was scowling at Elliott's back.

"Tucker's having fun."

Jase's gaze moved to follow mine where Tucker was sitting around the kitchen table playing some sort of drinking game. His head was thrown back in laughter, and I was genuinely happy that he was here. I missed him.

"He needs to relax. He works too hard."

"What about you?" I licked my dry lips. "Have you been working too hard too?" I watched him as his eyes stayed glued to my lips. "When are you going to have some fun?"

His gaze bounced back to mine. "I have plenty of fun."

I didn't let him see how badly those simple words affected me.

"Well, let's have some fun tonight."

His pupils flared, just slightly, but I noticed. When he didn't answer, I knew I would have to push him harder.

"Don't be a chicken." I threaded my fingers with his and tugged him away from the wall.

"Where are we going?" He set his cup down on the counter nearest him, but he didn't try to stop me.

"You'll see." I tightened my fingers and pulled him through the crowd of people that had all come out to celebrate my birthday. It didn't matter that they were all there though. The only thing that mattered was him.

He didn't hesitate as he followed me.

We walked out the back door, and as soon as the door closed behind us, the sound of the party cut off. It was only the two of us.

"You know there are bears and shit out here, right?" Jase asked as I led him to a trail that led through the trees at the edge of the backyard.

"Why, Jase Hale, are you scared?" I turned back to look at him, but I didn't dare let go of his hand. It was the first time he had ever let me touch him like this. It was the first time I had even dared.

"I'm smart." He smirked.

"My family has been coming to this cabin for as long as I can remember, and I have never seen a bear. Unless you think a squirrel might get us?" I bugged my eyes out as if I was truly scared.

"Very funny." He kicked a stick off the trail, and I laughed.

My parents' cabin sat practically on the top of a mountain, and they would die if they knew I was using it to throw a party. They thought that I went out with my girlfriends tonight and then planned to stay at one of their houses.

I felt guilty, but I wouldn't have this opportunity again.

I came to a stop when the trees thinned and all you could see were the stars in the sky. I dropped Jase's hand as I sat down on the ground, and I prayed that he would sit down beside me instead of taking off back toward the party.

I knew that he would rather be there.

But he didn't even seem to consider it.

He watched me as I leaned back on the ground and stared up at the sky then he joined me.

Our shoulders touched just barely, and neither of us spoke for several minutes as we listened to the quiet sounds of the world around us.

"So..." I hesitated, and I hated that I did. "Do you have any girlfriends at school?"

"Girlfriends?" He turned his head toward me, but I didn't meet his gaze. "As in plural?"

"Girlfriends. Girlfriend. Whichever." For some reason, the thought of him having one single girlfriend versus an entire volleyball team after him really bothered me.

"No." He chuckled and tucked his arm behind his head. "I'm still holding out for a set of twins to make my girlfriends dream come true."

I jabbed him in the side with my elbow and he rubbed the spot as his deep chuckle echoed through the air.

"What about you? Did the vultures come out as soon as your brother left?"

I laughed at the thought. Sure, I was pretty enough, but the thought that some guy was vying for the opportunity to get to me was laughable. My brother wasn't that scary.

"Oh yeah." I rolled my eyes. "They all came out of the woodwork as soon as Tucker crossed the county line."

"Figures." He said the word under his breath. "Why aren't you in there with one of them?" He hiked his thumb over his shoulder toward the direction of the cabin.

I rolled toward him and stared at the small scar that ran

just along the base of his chin. I wanted to touch it. I had wanted to touch it since the day I saw him crash his skateboard.

"Because I'm here with you."

He didn't move away from me as he had done so many times before. My forearm was pressed against his side, and I could smell him so clearly. He didn't smell like any other boy I knew. There was a slight hint of spicy cologne, but it was something below that pulled me in.

"We should get back." He said the words, but he didn't move.

I shook my head. "No one is missing us."

"Sophie." He said my name as if he was pained.

"Don't." I laid my hand on his chest. "Not tonight."

He stared at me then, really looked at me, and for the first time in my life, I loved what I saw in his eyes.

"What are you doing?" His voice was gruff and made my stomach tighten.

"Nothing I haven't done before." It was a lie. I had no damn clue what I was doing.

I just knew that I wanted to do it with him.

I had always wanted it to be with him.

Jase ran his hand down his face in frustration, and it was easy to see that he was warring with himself.

"Your brother." He looked back over his shoulder toward the cabin and my heart started hammering in my chest.

"Isn't here." I moved an inch closer to him before I reached up and hesitantly ran my finger over that small scar.

His eyes jerked back to mine.

He looked so serious, feuding with himself, and I felt a surge of excitement at the thought of challenging him. I wasn't the same little girl that he, my brother, and their friends used to pick on.

I let my fingers trail down his chin to the base of his neck and my breath caught as he swallowed down his nerves beneath them.

"Sophie." My name was a whisper on his lips, and I let them fuel me.

I pushed up on my knees and quickly draped one leg over his before he could stop me. I was straddling him, closer than I had ever been to him before, but he caught my hips in his hands before I could press them against his.

"What are you doing?" His voice was slightly panicked as he started to sit up, but that only moved his body closer to mine.

I let my arms fall to the top of his shoulders, and I couldn't miss the way his eyes stalked the rise and fall of my chest.

"I don't know," I answered honestly. "But please don't make me stop."

His eyes slammed shut, and I forced myself down against him despite the weak push of his hands against my hips. His hands tightened against me—the pressure of his fingertips against my skin unlike anything I had ever felt before.

His gaze met mine for only a moment before something inside of him snapped. I had been waiting for that shatter of his control for as long as I could remember.

He forced his hands into my hair as he jerked me forward—closing the tiny gap that remained between us, and he swallowed the sound of my shock with his lips against mine.

Everything around us fell away.

The first taste of his lips made me feel like I was starving.

That simple touch and I felt completely off-balance. I couldn't bring him close enough to me.

It wasn't at all what I had dreamed my first kiss with Jase would be like.

He was always in control. He was the flirt, the lady's man, but this Jase—he was as desperate as I was.

His hands fumbled over my body and his mouth crashed with mine. He bit my bottom lip and my hips pressed against his frantically.

I wasn't sure what I wanted from him, but I knew that I needed more.

His fingers tangled in my hair and I was surprised by how much my stomached tightened when he pulled my head back roughly. His mouth moved over my chin and down my neck, and I could feel his ravenousness in his kiss.

It only fueled my own need.

I moaned as I pressed my chest against his, and I prayed his tongue couldn't feel the rapid beat of my heart against my neck. I had no clue what I was doing, but it didn't matter.

Nothing mattered in that moment.

Jase's hand pushed the bottom of my t-shirt up my stomach, but he hesitated. I could feel the uncertainty in the falter of his touch and the shudder of his body beneath mine.

I didn't want him to be uncertain about me.

I couldn't stand it.

I brought my own hands to meet his at the bunched fabric of my shirt, and I pulled it over my head without a second thought.

He looked like he was in a daze as he took in my breasts, and I thanked God that I borrowed the tiny lace bra that was almost a full size too small for me from one of my friends. He wouldn't be looking at one of my white cotton bras with that same desire.

His finger dipped just inside the lace before he ran it along the edge. The rapid rise and fall of my chest came to a quivering halt as he leaned down, his gaze on mine, and ran his tongue against the thin fabric.

I could feel the hint of his tongue against my nipple, but it wasn't enough. I moved to drop the strap of my bra, but Jase quickly pushed my hand away. His teeth scraped against my nipple through the fabric, and I knew—I just knew that this was how I was going to die.

It was too much and not enough at the exact same time.

It was everything but just a taste.

He moved his mouth to the other breast, and my skin became covered in goose bumps as he blew the gentlest breath against the fabric he had just wet with his tongue.

My fingers wrapped in his hair, and I was almost embarrassed by the way I couldn't stop rolling my hips against his.

I had never felt like this before.

Not even close.

Not when I ran my own fingers against myself to try to figure out what this whole sex thing was all about and definitely not when I had been kissed by anyone else.

I tugged on the fabric of Jase's t-shirt, and he moved away from me only slightly to allow me to pull it over his head.

I didn't hesitate, I pressed my own mouth against his chest and tasted the skin that had probably been featured in too many teenage girls' dreams to count.

He groaned, low and deep, as my tongue ran over the base of his neck, and air hit my breasts as he slowly lowered my bra off my body. I pressed my naked chest against his, the feeling more than I knew it could be, and I cried out as he quickly flipped us. His body now hovering over mine.

He didn't unbutton my jeans as his finger slipped under the fabric and ran from one hip to the other. My stomach trembled under his touch, but I held my breath as he lowered his mouth and pressed a gentle kiss right below my belly button. I was so captivated by watching his mouth that I barely noticed his hand that slid beneath my jeans.

It wasn't until I felt the lightest touch against my center that my hips surged forward, and I had to bite my lip to stop myself from crying out.

Jase was working his way up my body with his mouth and his hand seemed to move with the same laziness as he pushed a finger through me and growled at the amount of wetness that he found.

I wanted to cover my face, but my arm was pinned under Jase's body. Instead, I let my fingers press against the front of his jeans.

He groaned, and his teeth scraped against the skin covering my collarbone.

When I felt how hard he was under my touch, I was no longer embarrassed by my own arousal.

He didn't give me time to worry about it anyway.

He began moving the heel of his hand against me in the tiniest circles, and I could barely remember my own name let alone any reason to be embarrassed.

Jase's mouth met mine and I gave him everything in my kiss as he took everything from my body. Our teeth clashed as we nipped at each other's lips. His tongue fought mine as I pushed my hips harder against his hand.

I was so close, so damn close, and I felt like I was going to break.

I was falling apart, I could feel it, but I didn't care.

Jase was holding onto me, and that was all that mattered.

I was surrounded by the smell of him, the taste of him was on my tongue, and I didn't care what happened next.

Until my brother's voice echoed through the trees around us. "Sophie!"

Jase's body tensed on top of mine, and I felt and saw his regret before he even uttered a word.

"Shit." He jerked his hand out of my pants and scrambled for his t-shirt just as he tossed my bra in my direction.

I held it against my chest, but I didn't make any move to put it on. I was too busy watching Jase. Watching him freak out. Watching him be a fucking coward.

There was no going back to what we just had.

"Sophie." My name was once again a whisper on his lips, but this time it was in panic. "Put your fucking clothes on."

I didn't do as he said.

I just sat there in complete shock at what had just happened. Not that I was about to hook up with Jase Hale, one of my brother's best friends and the guy I had been in love with for as long as I could remember.

I would never have regretted that.

Jase stood and dusted the dirt and leaves from his clothes as his gaze searched the tree line for my brother. He picked up my shirt and shook it out quickly before tossing it to me.

"Get dressed," he growled at me.

I slid my arms into my bra and slowly clasped it behind my back. Tucker's voice called out my name again, but I wasn't worried about my brother. This wasn't about him.

"Sophie." Jase started to pace. "I swear to God."

"Leave." I looked up at him. I didn't know what he saw when he looked down at me, but I knew my hair was still a mess from his hands and my skin was still burning from his touch. "Just go, Jase."

He stared down at me. There was conflict in his gaze. He didn't want to leave me, but he also didn't care about me enough to stay.

I could hear Tucker's footsteps as he made his way toward us, and I knew that Jase could too.

I wasn't being fair.

But neither was he.

None of it mattered though.

Because Jase took off in the opposite direction of Tucker, and I swore to myself that I would never let Jase Hale close enough to hurt me ever again.

CHAPTER 1
SOPHIE

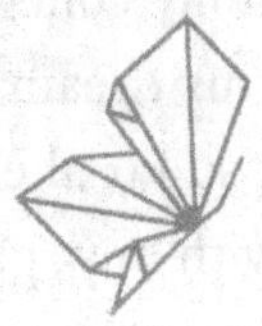

"Do you want to live with Mom and Dad forever?"

I slumped further into the couch cushions as I watched my brother sign some documents on his desk over FaceTime.

"Of course not."

I looked around the living room and prayed that he couldn't see the several bowls of ramen noodles that cluttered the coffee table. I was doing a good job hiding my hermit behaviors from my mom since she never came up to the over-garage apartment, but I didn't need Tucker sticking his nose where it didn't belong.

"Then you better get your ass to that interview tomorrow." He finally looked up from his paperwork to look at me.

I wished the couch would swallow me whole.

My interview.

I had managed to forget about the interview for all of five minutes, but my brother brought it right back to the forefront of my mind.

"I'm not going to miss the interview."

Even though I wanted to.

I wanted to be anywhere other than at that damn interview.

I had no experience and exactly zero prospects of a job other than this one.

And I meant zero.

I couldn't find a job in my college town, and no one was even close to interested in my dream city of Seattle.

I never really thought so far ahead to think that I would need to move back in with my parents after college but getting a job in my field apparently didn't happen overnight. Trust me, I started applying and trying to make connections six months before I graduated.

That wasn't something they really advertised in the college brochures.

There were several students that graduated with the same architecture degree as me that already had their jobs secured, but I didn't want to move just anywhere to get a job.

So, my options were pretty simple. I could move to Seattle like I had been dreaming of for as long as I could remember with no job and very little money and nowhere to live, or I could go home.

I had a feeling homeless and desperate would not be a good look on me. So, I settled for desperate and living with my parents.

My parents were thrilled to have me home. It had been four years since they had one of their children in their house.

But I had a feeling they were going to get over having me around if I didn't land a job soon. Being happy to cook your twenty-three-year-old daughter dinner every night could only last so long.

"Although, I don't know why I'm even wasting my time.

Jase isn't going to hire me. He's probably just going to sit across from me at his desk and love watching me beg for a job."

Tucker rolled his eyes and turned over another sheet of paper. Jase may have been his friend for the last thirteen years, but he was not a nice guy. At least not to me. He had proven that to me, and I was more than happy to keep our relationship exactly like it was—nonexistent.

"Stop being dramatic. He wouldn't have even given you an interview if he wasn't willing to take you seriously."

Oh, he was going to be serious alright. Serious about watching me grovel.

It was fine.

I was fine.

"Plus, he doesn't own the company. He may not even be the one to interview you."

"That would be awesome."

Tucker rolled his eyes again.

"He's not that bad." My brother looked up at me. "You two used to get along. Remember?"

Yeah. Until he ruined everything and didn't look back.

I didn't tell my brother that though.

I would never tell him.

"For sure." I nodded my head. "It will be fine."

Despite my nerves, I knew I couldn't miss the interview. My brother may have begged for the opportunity on my behalf, even though he said he didn't have to, but Jase still gave me an offer I couldn't refuse.

An interview.

One shot.

He didn't make any promises—he never had, but I just had to use the chance to wow him.

So tomorrow morning, I would sit across from him and pretend that he didn't intimidate the hell out of me. And while I was faking, I would pretend that I could work for the man who I hated without any complications whatsoever.

"Blow him away, sis."

And just like that, the only thing I could think about was what it would be like to bring Jase Hale to his knees.

No. This wouldn't be complicated at all.

CHAPTER 2
SOPHIE

I had tossed and turned all night.

I scoured the internet for possible questions Jase could ask me, but I had no doubt his questions wouldn't be listed there. He would probably come up with the most arbitrary things just to throw me off my game.

It didn't matter though.

I was as prepared as I could possibly be.

My black slacks were tight and made me feel like a million bucks. They were my power pants. Nothing could go wrong when I was in my power pants and a pair of black heels.

At least that was what I was telling myself.

I had looked up Norman Architecture while I lay in bed, and I had looked over every member of the team that was listed on the website. I wish I could say that there were more than two women mixed in with all of the men, but that would be a lie.

The trends of architecture and construction were state of the art and always on the rise, but it would appear that my gender wasn't a strong part of that. Out of my entire gradu-ating class, there were only ten females.

The only two listed on the Norman Architecture website was a receptionist by the name of Annie Jett and a young interior designer, Haley Brookes.

I'm only half embarrassed to admit that I stalked Haley on Facebook to see what she was like. She was gorgeous, that was obvious, and I hoped like hell she was nice.

If I was smart, I would have Facebook stalked Jase. But I refused. If I had been a good detective, I would have known that he was a big dog at Norman Architecture before I accepted the interview. My brother had failed to mention that small detail when he told me that a friend of his might have an opportunity for me. He knew I would have said no.

I should have said no.

But I was desperate.

It wasn't until he gave me the name of the company and told me that they were hiring for an associate architect that I figured out Jase was the one with the grand opportunity.

I could have killed my brother.

He didn't answer my phone calls when he realized that I had figured it out, but I called his fiancée, Kennedy, and ratted him out. Apparently, my brother's grand plan was to let me figure it out when I walked into the interview.

He was going to let me be blindsided.

Thank God, Jase's picture was front and center on their damn website.

I didn't even know that was what he had been doing with his life.

To be honest, I had avoided knowing anything about him that I could. Out of sight, out of mind. At least, that was my plan.

Turns out, I'm not the best planner.

The front door to Norman Architecture was heavy and masculine, and if I hadn't pounded a double shot of espresso right before I got here, I would have been intimidated.

But I pulled that door open with a smile on my face, and I breathed a sigh of relief when the receptionist, Annie, smiled up at me.

"Hi." I waved at her awkwardly. "I have an interview scheduled with Mr. Hale." I almost choked on the formal words. "I'm Sophie Moore."

"Hi, Sophie." She patted the back of her head where her grey hair was pulled up into a chignon and pulled out a pen that was tucked there. "I'm Annie."

She marked my name out on a planner that rested on the desk in front of her.

"It's nice to meet you."

"You too, doll." She looked completely sincere. "If you'll have a seat, I'll let Jase know you're here. It should only be a couple minutes."

I nodded my head and took a seat in the reception area as she disappeared down a hallway. I set my bag on the ground and flexed my hands to keep them from shaking. I didn't know if it was the caffeine or adrenaline, but I couldn't let either get to me.

It was only a moment later when Jase walked out of the same hallway that Annie had just left through, and I didn't miss the way she laughed at something he said as she trailed behind him.

The smile on his face dropped as soon as his eyes met mine.

"Sophie." He nodded his head toward me, and I quickly grabbed my bag and stood.

"Hi, Jase." I took a step toward where he stood, and I couldn't stop myself from letting my gaze run over his dark blue jeans and white button-down shirt. His sleeves were rolled up to his elbows, and it was clear that he had already been deep in his work.

He waved his hand for me to follow him, and I realized that was the extent of pleasantries we were going to extend to each other.

His office was nice, most of the space taken up by a massive desk that was covered in different folders and papers. A bit of organized chaos.

I took a seat across from him as he sat down in the large chair behind his desk. The wall behind him was covered in windows, and I wondered how often he stared out at the view to work through his problems.

"Did you bring your resume?" He shifted in his seat impatiently.

"Of course." I pulled the file with my resume and letters of recommendation out of my bag and handed it to him.

He opened it, flipping the pages without saying a word, and I prayed that the world would open up and swallow me whole.

His hair was shorter than the last time I saw him. It had been, I don't know, eight months ago at the opening of my brother's bar. He looked exactly the same but so different. His green eyes though. They were the same.

"The position is for an associate architect position. You will be a part of a team that consists of three other members, and you will answer directly to your team manager."

I nodded my head. He said it as if he figured it would be an issue.

"Can you handle that?"

"Of course, I can handle that." I had to stop myself from rolling my eyes or grabbing the stapler off his desk and throwing it at his head. "I'm not some errant child."

There was a soft ding on his computer, and he turned toward it without acknowledging anything I had just said. His fingers tapped against his keyboard as his eyes scanned over the screen. He took his time answering something on his computer that was clearly more important than my interview before he lazily turned back to me.

"Let's cut to the chase, Sophie. You are by far the most qualified applicant that we've had." The words were killing him to say out loud. I could practically taste the bitterness on my own tongue. "I don't need to waste either of our time by asking you a bunch of bullshit interview questions."

I tensed, and I could feel my cheeks heating. I would be humiliated if he brought me in here only to not even give me a chance.

"I told Tucker you would do this." I straightened in my seat. "If you weren't even considering giving me the job, then why the hell did you even agree to the interview."

He sat back in his seat and stared at me. One hand rubbed gently across his chin, right over his scar, as he flipped a pencil in his other, but his gaze didn't move away from me. I was on fire under his stare, and I swear I could have felt it even with my eyes closed.

That was the thing about Jase. He had always known how to burn me.

"I agreed to this interview." He pushed his chair out from his desk and stood.

My breath caught in my throat as he made his way toward me. We were close enough already. There was no reason for him to stop right in front of me and lean against his desk. He was too potent this close. Too intimidating.

"Because I was planning on giving you the job."

I blinked at his words.

"You were?" Hope bloomed in my chest.

He nodded his head. "It's not a good idea though."

And just like that, it disappeared.

"Why not?" I knew why not, God, I knew—but I needed to hear him say it.

He stared straight at me and didn't even flinch as he said the next words. "I don't usually hire my former hookups."

I swallowed hard but refused to allow him to see how his words affected me.

His words were harsh, but I probably deserved them.

After that night, I had made it perfectly clear to him that he was nothing more to me.

A drunken hookup.

"You're not the only man that's had his hand in my pants, Jase. I think I can handle being professional around you."

I watched his fingers tighten around the edge of the desk.

"I am not your friend while you're here." He stood up a little straighter. "And I'm not some notch on your bedpost. I'm your boss."

He stood to his full height, and I had to lean my head back to look up at him.

"Should I call you sir?" I didn't know why I said it. He was going to give me a job. I just had to figure out how to keep my big mouth shut.

His smirk made me squeeze my thighs together involuntarily, but he noticed. Of course, he noticed.

"That'd be a good start." He leaned down closer to me,

and I was overwhelmed by the smell of his cologne. He smelled so different than he used to. "And drop the sass."

I opened my mouth to tell him exactly where he could shove my sass when he pressed the intercom button on his office phone.

Annie's voice came through the speaker. "Yep?"

"Can you get Ms. Moore a new employee packet?"

"Yes!" She sounded excited, and I realized that I had reason to be too.

"Thank you." Jase lifted his finger from the button and his office went silent again.

"Be here at eight tomorrow morning, and Annie will introduce you to your team."

"Thank you, Jase." I stood from my chair and grabbed my bag. We were only about a foot apart from each other, and I had the urge to put my arms around him. It was an urge I hadn't felt in a very long time. I took a step back. "You won't regret this."

He ran his fingers through his hair as I made my way toward his door. I had barely pulled it open when he finally spoke again. "Don't make me."

CHAPTER 3
JASE

This was going to be a disaster.

Sophie Moore didn't belong here.

Not as my employee.

Not as my friend.

Not as anything.

I couldn't tell Tucker no though. What would I have said?

"Sorry, man. Your sister and I haven't gotten along since I ran after finger-banging her on her eighteenth birthday."

That would have gone over really well.

Although, I didn't run. Not like she thought I did. I panicked. Tucker would have hated me, fucking hated me, if he had seen me with her. He would have killed me.

And I knew what kind of pussy that made me. I was perfectly clear on that fact. But I wasn't willing to lose my best friend in the world.

Sophie made it clear that it wasn't worth it.

When I moved to the edge of the trees and watched her pull her t-shirt over her head, I almost went right back to her. I didn't want to hurt her. It was the last thing I wanted, but Tucker came out of the tree line and Sophie leaned back on her elbows and stared up at him with a smile.

"What are you doing?" Tucker sat down beside her.

"Just slumming it up here in the woods." She looked over to where I had just left. I knew she couldn't see me, but I could see her.

I wanted to kiss the shit out of her and throttle her at the exact same time.

She had every right to be pissed at me, but her words affected me just the same.

I tried to talk to her once they got back to the cabin. I couldn't leave things as they were. I wouldn't be able to live with it. Sophie had been a part of my life for a long time.

It didn't matter what just happened. I wouldn't let that change.

When I found her, her arms were wrapped around the neck of some douchebag I didn't know but definitely didn't like.

"Can we talk?" I rubbed my hand down the back of my neck.

"About what?" She grinned at me before she took another sip of her drink.

She had clearly been pounding back the drinks since she and Tucker made their way back. It somehow made me angrier at her.

"About us?" I practically growled at her.

"You and my brother, us?" She tightened her arm around that asshole's neck and his eyes immediately went to her chest that was pressed against him. "Surely that can wait." Her hand ran along the edge of his t-shirt, and I was seconds away from punching him in the face when I watched her finger dip under the neckline.

"Sophie, I'm not playing."

Her gaze jerked up to mine and the playful, drunk Sophie was gone. "Neither am I."

We stared at each other, and I hated that her hands were still on him.

"I don't have time for your shit, Jase." I swear she moved the tiniest bit closer to him. "Elliott here was just about to give me a birthday present."

She smiled up at him and I hated her in that moment.

But she wasn't here to reminisce about our past. She was here for a job, and I offered it to her.

I wasn't lying when I said that she was the most qualified out of all the applicants we had. There had been exactly five people to apply. Two of them didn't even have the correct degrees let alone talent.

She would do well. I knew that. I wasn't stupid.

It was at what expense she would do well that was my concern.

Because I gave her the job, but I wasn't going to completely stick my neck out for her. If she wanted to succeed here, then she was going to have to do that on her own.

I thought about the team she was going to be a part of, and I couldn't stop myself from smiling. It was a dick move— one hundred percent, but I wasn't the one who told her to apply when the only position we had open was with a team leader who was a bigger asshole than I could even think about being.

Tom was old enough to be my dad, and I was pretty sure

he spent at least half of those years studying the art of getting under other people's skin.

But he was a damn good architect.

He could teach Sophie things that almost no one else in this company could.

If she could hang.

When it came to him, you either sank or swam. There was no in-between.

"That Sophie seems sweet."

I looked up at Annie as she made her way into my office.

"You never were a very good judge of character, Annie."

She rolled her eyes and laid some papers down on my desk. "Mr. Norman will like her. She was a good decision."

"I wish he'd get his ass back here." I ran my fingers through my hair. "How long do you normally take off after a hip replacement?"

I was joking, but I also wasn't. Mr. Norman owned Norman Architecture, and he had left me in charge while he was gone. It was a responsibility I didn't want nor was I ready for.

"He'll be back in a few more weeks. He needs to take it easy." Annie marked a paper with a tab indicating I needed to sign it. "Speaking of, are you going to leave this office before the sun goes down any time soon?"

She wasn't wrong. I had spent far too much time here lately, but I felt like I couldn't get caught up.

Work, eat, and sleep.

They had been the only three things that mattered since Mr. Norman put me in charge.

I didn't even have time to fuck.

But I didn't need to think about that with Annie in my office. I would probably give her a heart attack.

"I've been busy." I shrugged my shoulders.

"I know you have." She patted my forearm. Annie was the unofficial mom of the office, and she took her job seriously when it came to me. "That Grace girl keeps calling for you. Maybe you should leave early and take her out to dinner."

I winced.

I hadn't spoken to Grace since the night I left her apartment before she woke up. What was that? Three weeks ago?

Shit. I really needed to get laid.

"I'll think about it." I nodded my head. "I told Sophie to meet up with you in the morning. Will you show her around and introduce her to Tom?"

She sneered up her tiny nose. "You know I don't like talking to that man."

"I know." I grinned. "But Sophie still has to meet him."

She shook her head as if that was the worst idea she had ever heard as she moved back around the front of my desk. "Sophie seems too sweet for Tom. Maybe you should put her somewhere else."

"There's nowhere else to put her," I reminded her. "She'll do fine."

Annie stared at me for a moment as if I had lost my mind. "You don't like her much, do you?"

"She's fine." I gritted out the words as I signed one of the papers she had put in front of me before handing it to her. "She's one of my best friends' little sister, and I've known her forever."

I signed the next paper.

"Huh."

My gaze snapped up to Annie.

"Huh, what?"

"Nothing." She shook her head and a few pieces of her grey hair slipped out of the knot at the back of her head and a small smile formed on her lips.

"I don't care about her one way or another." I was trying to make myself perfectly clear. "She needed a job, and she's qualified."

"Whatever you say, boss man." Annie gathered the papers I had just signed in her arms and turned back toward the door.

"There's nothing there," I called out to her as she stepped out into the hall.

She flicked her hand in the air, basically telling me to piss off.

I ran my fingers through my hair and knew with one hundred percent certainty that I was right.

This was going to be a disaster.

CHAPTER 4
SOPHIE

I was nervous as hell.

I had all the normal first-day jitters, but they were intensified by the fact that I had a fitful sleep last night filled with dreams of Jase.

I woke up in a panic.

Would I see him constantly at work?

I hoped not.

Accepting a job from him was fine. I could handle that, but I definitely didn't want to deal with him hovering over me the entire time.

I wouldn't be able to concentrate.

The office was relatively quiet when I walked in, but Annie was already at her desk working away on her computer. She looked up and smiled when she saw me walk in.

"Sophie! Hi!"

Her enthusiasm at seeing me made my nerves calm down just slightly.

"Hi." I adjusted my bag on my shoulder. "Jase told me to meet up with you this morning."

"Of course." She stapled some papers together before standing up. "Let me show you around."

I followed behind her as she led me down the same hallway that took us to Jase's office for my interview. I tried my hardest not to let my eyes linger too long on his closed office door. Was he in there?

"So." Annie looked back at me over her shoulder. "Did you grow up here?"

"Yeah." I nodded my head. "My parents live about five minutes away from here actually. I moved away for college, but I moved back." I shrugged my shoulders.

"This is the break room."

She stopped at a door and I peeked in around her. It was pretty standard with a fridge, sink, and a long kitchen countertop. There were two round tables in the middle of the room, and I absently wondered if Jase took his lunch break in here.

"Make sure you put your name on anything you put in the fridge. We have some food thieves around here." She narrowed her eyes down the hall as if she could see the culprit.

"Got it." I laughed softly.

"Your office is right down here." She moved away from the break room and led a bit farther down the hall. "Let's get you settled in there then I'll introduce you to your team."

She opened the door to my office, and I was surprised by the amount of space I was given. It was significantly smaller than Jase's, but it was more than enough for me.

There was a large wooden desk in the center of the room

with three large windows behind it. The room was flooded with natural light, and I couldn't stop myself from smiling.

"This is my office?" I looked over at Annie who was already looking at me.

"Yup." She moved farther into my office and ran her hand over my desk. "You can decorate it however you want, and I'll let you into my supply closet after you meet your team, so you can get what you need."

I looked down at the two large computer monitors that sat on the left side of my desk, and I knew that the software on there was going to be better than anything I had ever used before.

"That sounds perfect."

Annie reached into her pocket and pulled out a small gold key. "Here is the key to your office. The only other people who have access are me, Mr. Hale, and Mr. Norman. If you want to leave your bag in here, I'll take you to your team."

I smiled even though she just said Jase had full access to my office and set my bag down in my chair. I straightened my blouse and tucked a stray piece of hair behind my ear.

"Okay." I took a deep breath.

The rest of my team wasn't very far away from my office. Apparently, there were three others on my team, all men, and we would work on different projects together.

Annie smiled as she talked about them, but I watched the way her face faltered when she talked about my team leader, Tom.

I wanted to ask her about it, but it was too late. She rapped her knuckles against an office door, and I could hear muffled talking before the door cracked open. The man standing in front of me smiled. His dark beard took up most of his face, surrounding his warm smile.

"Hey, Annie."

"Hey, Sean. This is Sophie Moore. She's going to be joining your team."

Sean stuck his hand in my direction. "Hi, Sophie. I'm Sean."

I placed my hand in his and returned his firm shake. "It's nice to meet you, Sean." I wasn't lying either. Sean seemed nice, and I took a calming breath for the first time since I walked in the doors of Norman Architecture.

"You too." He opened the door wider, and I caught a glimpse of two other men in the office.

The man sitting behind the desk didn't bother looking up from his work. His light grey hair was in disarray as if he had been running his fingers through it, and his hands appeared to be covered in so much lead that I knew he probably lived with a drafting pencil in his hand.

The other man quickly stood from his seat. He was rail thin with blond hair pushed out of his face, and he smiled a bit awkwardly as he reached his hand out to me.

"I'm Darren."

His hand was clammy in mine, but I returned his handshake just the same.

"Nice to meet you, Darren. I'm Sophie."

He nodded his head once then looked back at his chair like he was dying to get back there.

Annie left me with my new teammates but promised she would find me in a bit to see how I was settling in. She said it loud enough for the entire team to hear, and it may have just been my imagination, but it sounded like there was a bit of threat in her voice.

The man behind the desk told me that his name was Tom, but that was the extent of introduction that I got from him. He didn't seem too interested in finding out anything about me either.

I sat down in the empty chair closest to Sean.

"We're busy," Tom said out loud, and I was unsure if his comment was directed at me or just in general. "We have to wrap up the Collins Residential Project so we can work on the bid for the Anderson Development."

I quickly wrote a few notes in the notebook I brought in with me, but they made absolutely no sense. I didn't have a clue what project they were working on or what project they were bidding on. My notes consisted of a bunch of words.

Collins Residential Project.

Busy.

Anderson Development.

Kill me now.

Doodle heart.

"This bid is huge for us." Tom finally looked up from his work to look at us. Well, to look at them I should say. "Jase has every team within the company working on it."

He passed out a stack of papers to Darren and Sean, and finally me. I had to stand a bit to reach his outreached hand. He started talking again before I could sit back down.

"You have all the details of the project in front of you. I'd like each of you to work on this in your spare time until we complete the Collins project. Then we'll come together and see what we've come up with."

I nodded my head, but Tom's gaze came straight to me.

"Sophie."

Wow. He actually heard my name.

"I know this will be a lot to walk into. I'd like for you to focus on helping the three of us with things we need to help get ready for this project."

He wanted me to be their glorified assistant.

I looked over at Sean and Darren, but both of them had their heads down looking over the paperwork Tom had just given them.

"Okay." I barely managed to let the word slip past my lips.

He held out a much bigger stack in my direction.

I took the papers and looked down at the stack of building codes, fire regulations, zoning laws, and city ordinances.

"Those are for the Anderson Development." He pointed at the stack that now rested in my lap. "I need you to go over those with a fine-tooth comb. We need to know exactly what we're working with."

It would take me forever to get through that stack, but I wouldn't let him see that he was bothering me in any way.

"Got it." I smiled at him.

His eyes narrowed slightly, almost involuntarily, before he turned back to the work in front of him.

"Alright. Let's get busy."

Sean and Darren quickly stood and made their way out of the office. I didn't waste any time in following them. Spending extra time with Tom wasn't anywhere near my wish list.

"He's not always that bad," Sean said quietly as we walked back in the direction of my office.

"Bad day?" I laughed softly and tucked a piece of hair behind my ear.

He winced just a tiny bit. "Not exactly." He shook his head. "But sometimes he has really good days."

I laughed. "So, wait for a really good one before asking for anything."

"Exactly." He chuckled. "Or just be prepared."

I smiled and tried to not let my anxiety show.

"This is me." He stopped by an office door that was a few down from mine. "Let me know if you need anything."

"Thanks." I kept walking and made my way toward the break room that Annie had shown me. If I was going to make it through the rest of the day, I was in desperate need for coffee.

I could see Jase's office and noticed that his door was cracked just a bit. I hated myself for doing it, but I craned my head and tried to catch a peek inside as I leaned against the break room doorway.

"Looking for something?"

I jumped so hard that I managed to drop at least half of the stack of papers in my hands.

"Oh my God." My gaze shot up to Jase for only a second before I dropped to my knees in front of him and started gathering the papers in a haphazard stack. I prayed that these pages were numbered, or I would never manage to get them back in order.

Jase's deep chuckle made my back straighten, and I hated the way I felt when I looked up at him. Was it possible that he was even more handsome than usual today?

He squatted down in front of me and his deep blue slacks tightened around his thighs. Not that I actually cared about his thighs, but it was too hard not to notice.

His hands reached out to help me pick up the mess I had made, and I hated that he was seeing the assignment that Tom had given me. Not that he couldn't just ask me. He was my boss after all. He was probably the one to tell Tom to treat me like I was an idiot.

It didn't matter though. I would prove them both wrong.

"I'm sorry." I put the stack of papers that were now bent and out of order on top of the papers I had managed not to drop and quickly stood back up.

"Were you"—he looked out the break room door like I had only moments before—"trying to look into my office?"

"What?" I sounded outraged and completely guilty. "Absolutely not." I shook my head. "I was trying to see if Annie was busy. She told me to find her after my meeting with my team."

He arched an eyebrow at me. "You can't see Annie's desk from here."

"Obviously." I tightened my grip on my papers. "Why do you think I was leaning back."

"Uh huh." He rubbed his hand over his chin. "How did meeting your team go?"

"It was good," I lied.

"Yeah?" He knew it too.

"For sure." I nodded my head. "Everyone was great."

"Good." He smiled at me, and it was a smile that I had loved for far too many years.

"Well, I better get to work." I backed out of the break room and didn't give him a chance to say anything else. I quickly made my way to my office with the small amount of dignity I had left and no damn coffee.

CHAPTER 5
JASE

I hadn't seen Sophie in four days.

I would love to say that I had just been busy, but the truth was that I was avoiding her.

She had been working here for less than a week, and already, I was letting her get under my skin. The shitty thing was that I wasn't sure if she was doing it on purpose. It was just who she was.

Our entire company was piled into the conference room for our meeting today. We needed to talk about the Anderson Development. This project would be huge. Not only for the architect who designed it but for our entire company.

But we were only one of several companies who would be working our asses off to land this job, we just had to work the hardest.

I didn't care how many late nights I had to spend around here.

I know that everyone in the conference room was watching me, but I couldn't help watching Sophie as she walked into the room alone. Her gaze bounced around the room and it was easy to see how anxious she was as her gaze finally landed on Sean. She quickly made her way over to him, and I watched her ass the entire way.

I wasn't the only one either.

She was wearing some tight-ass skirt that showed off her ass a little too fucking well, and I made a mental note to ask Annie if she gave her an employee handbook. We didn't have a ton of women around the office, and I had never once had to worry about what Annie was wearing, but I was sure there is some sort of dress code in there.

And that skirt she was wearing definitely went against it.

She leaned her back against the wall since every chair in the room was already taken. I almost bit the heads off of all of my guys since they were sitting on their lazy asses while making a woman stand. In heels, no less.

Heels that made her legs look impossibly long.

Are heels against our dress code?

Annie laid a piece of paper in front of me, and I finally pulled my attention away from Sophie. The paper was blank, nothing more than something to bring my attention back to where it needed to be, and I realized that Annie had just caught me ogling my new employee.

She smiled at me. Not a sweet motherly smile that you would expect out of her, but a smile that told me that we're going to talk about this later.

I loved Annie.

More than just about anyone else at this place, but I didn't want to talk to her about Sophie.

"Alright." My voice rang out through the room and all the quiet murmuring stopped. "As you all know, we are bidding on the Anderson Development in four weeks. That means that we have four weeks to come up with a design that is going to blow everyone else out of the water."

I looked down at the plans in front of me.

"This job will be our biggest one yet. I want everyone spending their every spare minute working on this. Every team will come up with a design and Mr. Norman and I will decide which bid we'll go with. Four weeks."

I held up four fingers and glanced in Sophie's direction. She was staring straight at me.

"I know that isn't a lot of time."

"That's no time," Tom grumbled from his spot at the table.

I let my gaze slide to him before I continued.

"But it is all the time we have."

I stared at him and dared him to speak again. That fucker was talented, but he loved testing my patience. He loved testing everyone's.

"If you need anything, my door is always open. Now let's make Mr. Norman proud."

A few of the men smiled and a few of them grumbled, but I didn't care. We were going to win this bid whether they grumbled about it or not.

Most of the men flocked to the muffins Annie had brought in for the meeting, but I knew that she had some set aside for me somewhere. She always did.

Instead, I made my way toward Sophie.

"Have you had time to look at the requests?" Tom had stepped into my path and didn't care where I was going.

"I have." I nodded and looked down at the paper in front of him which I had read more times than I can count.

"It's a bit excessive."

"It's what they want." I shrugged my shoulders.

"What does Dan think of it?" He was referring to Mr. Norman, and I knew he only brought him up because he wanted to remind me that this wasn't my company.

"Mr. Norman hasn't even looked over it yet. He's resting."

Tom tsked under his breath and rubbed at his jaw. I was about to make my way around him when he opened his mouth again.

"This new one you put on my team."

My gaze jumped back to Sophie who was talking to a few people around her.

"I'm not sure about her."

"You're not sure about anyone." I meet his stare. "That's why I have to hire someone new for your team every few months. She's on your team whether you like it or not."

I watched him grind his teeth instead of biting back at me. He wanted to yell at me, to tell me where to shove everything I had just said, but he couldn't. I was his boss, and that chapped his ass most of all.

"We'll see how she does." He had to get this last word in before he turned and walked away. I let him. It wasn't worth my breath.

I searched the room for Sophie, but she was already making her way out of the room.

I cursed Tom for that.

I fielded a few more questions before I finally made my way out of the packed conference room. Sophie's office door was closed as I made my way past. I hesitated near it and contemplated raising my hand and knocking, but I didn't actually have anything I needed to say to her.

Maybe I would have Annie talk to her about her skirt or maybe I'd actually read the fucking handbook first.

I was about to walk away. One foot was literally in the air to move away from her when her office door opened.

"Jase." She startled at seeing me outside her office.

Hell, I was shocked myself.

"Sophie." I nodded toward her and started moving away from her as if I had only been walking by.

She knew I wasn't.

"I actually wanted to talk to you." She leaned against her doorway, and my gaze instantly followed her legs as she crossed her ankles.

It was that fucking skirt.

"I need to request off for all of Tucker and Kennedy's wedding activities in three weeks." She looked down the hall to where Tom's office stood. "Do I need to go through Tom for that or do I go directly through you?"

She looked like she was nervous to ask me, but at least she thought I was less of an asshole than Tom.

"I'll take care of it." Have her hips always curved that way? "I'll be off the same days."

"Of course." She tucked a piece of hair behind her ear before crossing her arms. Her breasts pushed up slightly higher by the movement. I usually wasn't so thrown off my game by a simple pair of breasts, but I had these particular breasts in my mouth before. I knew what they tasted like. At least I used to. I wondered if they would taste differently now or if they'd be exactly as I remembered.

"Well." She straightened to her full height. "I better get back to work." She brought her hand to her lips as if she was telling a secret. "My boss is a bit of a dick."

I hated that I smiled. It used to be so damn easy to smile around her.

"Which one?"

She grinned at me, and it had been so long since I had seen that look on her face. It hit me then how much I missed it. How much I had hated the time where we had hated each other.

"Wouldn't you like to know?" She winked at me.

Fucking winked.

Then she closed her office door as if I didn't have a key.

CHAPTER 6
SOPHIE

Work sucked.

Actually, let me rephrase that.

Tom sucked.

He was smart. I could spot that easily as I reviewed his work for *minor errors* as he had instructed me to do.

Apparently, there would be no major errors to be found.

To be fair, I barely found any minor ones.

I was excited to see what he put together for the Anderson Development. That damn development was the only thing I worked on. Not actually worked on, but you know, did administrative work for Tom on.

But I now knew that project like the back of my hand.

The Anderson Development was going to be an entire shopping center at the edge of our growing town that consisted of thirty shops and four restaurants. The developers had very specific ideas for the build. They wanted it to have a quaint, small-town feel.

They didn't want it to look like they took a plot of land and built over thirty shops on it while doing exactly that.

Their requirements almost seemed impossible, but I liked them.

Actually, the more I thought about them, I loved them.

I had been thinking about them a lot too. I had spent the last several days putting together a massive report for Tom which included all of the fire codes, city ordinances, and any other regulations we must follow, and I had spent so much time looking over it that I dreamed about the project when I slept and daydreamed about it when I was awake.

My mother was already worried that I was working too much, but my mom always worried. Sometimes I didn't even feel like I was back living with my parents since I typically worked too late to actually spend time with them.

"Do you have that report ready?"

I looked up at Tom as he took a seat in the chair across from my desk.

"Yes." I grabbed one of the four reports I had printed off and bound in a project folder and handed it to him.

He quickly flipped through it. His face gave nothing away other than the fact that he seemed pissed off twenty-four seven.

"I need this formatted differently." He picked up a pen off my desk and started scribbling on the paper. "This will make it a lot easier to work with when we start planning tomorrow."

He could have told me that from the beginning.

"You'll understand once you start designing."

I had to bite my tongue to not ask him when that would be. I was hired as an associate architect, not his personal assistant.

"Okay." It was the only thing I could manage.

He tossed the folder down on my desk in front of me,

and I could already see the blur of his corrections through the clear plastic of the folder.

"We need those by tomorrow." He stood up and I glanced at the clock. It was already six o'clock and there was no telling how long his corrections would take me. "I'll see you in the morning."

"Goodnight." I gritted the word through my teeth.

"Night." He didn't even glance back at me as he picked up his jacket off the back of the chair and headed in the direction of the front door.

I took a deep breath and ran my fingers through my hair before I dared open that damn folder.

There were more marks on the paper than printed ink, and I could barely decipher what anything said.

I opened a new document on my computer before kicking my heels off in the corner of the room. I pulled the rubber band from my bun and let my hair fall down my back. I already had a headache without the help of my topknot, and nobody else would be here this late.

It didn't really matter what I looked like.

I scoured over Tom's notes and tried to decode what format he wanted this in exactly. I made little notes on a scrap piece of paper and growled in frustration when the words that he wrote made absolutely no sense.

My phone lighting up was a welcome distraction, and I quickly clicked on the message that popped across from my screen.

Kennedy: Don't forget that your final dress fitting is on Wednesday at 6PM.

I wanted to tell her that I hoped I will be out of work on time to go, but I don't.

She was the bride for Christ's sake. She didn't need anything else causing her stress.

Me: I'll be there!

My brother's wedding was just a few weeks away, and I couldn't wait until they got here. I needed a small reprieve from work. Even if it was just a few days.

Most of my friends from high school had either moved away or were now three kids deep. Not that I minded kids but trying to correlate my schedule with a busy momma was starting to look impossible.

The only people I had hung out with in Tennessee outside of work were my parents. I was pathetic, but at least they were good company.

I tapped my finger against my keyboard. I didn't even know where to start. Halsey. She always managed to put me in a better mood.

I minimized that blank document that was staring into my soul and quickly pulled up Spotify. Halsey was playing through my speakers within seconds, and I instantly felt a little more at peace.

I pulled the document back up and stared down at Tom's notes. I turned Halsey up just a few more notches.

I started typing what I hoped was what Tom wanted, and let Halsey keep me sane. I sang along with her about all these damn men who had been letting us both down.

I must have been so into it that I didn't hear when he entered my office.

I didn't hear him take a seat in the chair across from my desk, and I didn't feel him watching me.

It wasn't until I smelled a hint of his spicy cologne that I looked up from what I was doing.

My hand flew to my mouth. "How long have you been there?"

I quickly tapped the volume button on my keyboard to quiet Halsey before she dropped a few more F-bombs or talked about giving messy head.

"A few minutes." Jase's white button-up shirt was rolled at the sleeves and his green eyes were staring straight at me.

"I'm sorry." I pushed away from my desk a bit, but I had no idea what I was doing. My heels were in the corner and I had thrown my rubber band across the room like some sort of bra burner.

"What for?" The corner of his mouth tipped up into a smile. "You were putting on a good show."

"Ha ha." I wasn't laughing. "I didn't realize anyone else was here."

I tucked my hair that I was sure looked like a hot damn mess behind my ear.

"I'm here." He let his hands rest on his stomach as he leaned back in the chair, and I had a momentary lapse in judgment as I wondered if he still had perfectly sculpted abs under that shirt.

"Obviously." I let my gaze drop down to Tom's notes and winced. Of course, his gaze followed mine.

"What does Tom have you working on so late?" He leaned forward to look at the mess in front of me.

"Well." I didn't want to show him. I didn't want him to see how terribly Tom thought I was doing. "Apparently, the code and ordinance report I did for him wasn't in the correct format. Although, I'm still not sure what format he wants me to put it in."

Jase nodded before quickly standing and making his way around my desk.

"What are you doing?" I asked as he grabbed my computer mouse and moved closer to me than he had been in what seemed like forever.

"You do know that I was a newbie here once upon a time too, right?" He looked over at me, and he was so close that his shoulder brushed against mine with the movement.

"I assumed you just walked right in and owned the place." I couldn't stop myself from getting a little dig at him. He may have been helping me, but it was a hard habit to break.

He rolled his eyes and turned his attention back to the computer. I watched as his fingers moved across my keyboard and mouse. The muscles of his forearms bunched and tightened with the movement, and for the first time in my life, I found myself insanely attracted to a man's forearms.

His forearms.

I needed to put some space between us.

"Here you go." He clicked open a document and stood. "This is the template for the format Tom is wanting."

I looked over the screen at the template he had just opened. It made complete and total sense, but it didn't match anything on Tom's notes.

"His notes though..." I trailed off and looked down at the notes in front of me.

"Are shit. He expects you to be able to read his mind."

I looked back up at the screen and down at the notes again. "But..."

"Trust me." Jase moved back around my desk. "You hungry? I ordered a pizza."

I stared at him like he was crazy. He knew I loved pizza.

"Yeah." I nodded my head.

"Cool." He checked his phone. "It should be here any minute. I'll be back in a few."

I tried to keep my jaw from hitting the ground as Jase walked out of my office. This was the nicest he had been to me in a long time. Hell, it was the nicest we had been to each other.

It was stupid really.

Our dislike for each other.

We were kids.

Stupid, infatuated (on my part) kids who had no business doing anything together. I wasn't the same girl that I was back then. Jase wasn't the same guy either.

But there was something about hating him that made everything easier.

Hating him was safe. It was what we had been doing for too many years now, but I could admit to myself and only myself that I did miss being friends with him.

But I fucked that all up.

By the time he made it back into my office, I had managed to get the report about three-quarters of the way finished. His template was a damn lifesaver, and I quickly copied and pasted parts from my report to his.

Jase had a large pizza in one hand and a six-pack of beer in the other.

"I didn't know pizza places delivered beer." I looked up at him like he had lost his damn mind.

"They don't, but the little shop down the street sells it." He shrugged.

"We cannot drink at work," I whispered like someone was going to jump out of the shadows and fire us both on the spot.

"It's technically not work hours."

I looked down at the clock, and he was right. It was almost seven thirty.

"Plus, the boss and I are pretty tight." His grin was contagious. It always had been even when I hated it.

I still hated it.

He popped the top of one of the beers and handed it to me.

"If I get fired, I'm blaming you." I pointed the neck of my beer in his direction before bringing it to my lips.

"You usually do."

I could tell that he didn't mean to say that out loud. Not that he actually showed his emotions, but his mouth drew up at the side and quickly pulled his lip into his teeth.

I swallowed the tart beer and tried not to let him see how much his words affected me. "That's true."

His eyebrows rose in shock. "You're admitting that you blame me." He put his hand on his chest dramatically.

"Well." I threw open the lid to the pizza box. "To be fair, it usually is your fault."

He grabbed a slice of the hot pizza and took a bite without even waiting for it to cool. "You said usually. That means I'm not always to blame."

"Not always." I shook my head then stuffed my own mouth with pizza. He had gotten pepperoni which meant that he thought of me when he ordered. I knew for a fact that his favorite pizza was meat lovers.

It was sweet, but I didn't call him out.

"Are you excited for the wedding?" I didn't know what else to say. We hadn't spent this much time together one-on-one in a long time.

"Oh yeah." He took a sip of his beer. "Wedding season is my favorite season."

"I could see that." I licked some sauce off my thumb. "I bet the ladies go crazy for you in a suit."

He grinned which told me I wasn't wrong. It also didn't make my chest ache just the tiniest bit.

"Like you can talk. I'm surprised you aren't married yet."

I almost choked on my pizza.

I chugged my beer to help clear my throat. "Yeah. That won't be happening *any* time soon."

He chuckled. "You're full of it."

I twirled a string of cheese that was hanging off my pizza around my finger before bringing it into my mouth. "Nope. I don't even have any options."

"I bet you find loads of options at the wedding." He cocked an eyebrow. "I bet that you get asked out far before I do at this thing."

I really take a good look at him. If he had made that bet a few years ago, I would have said hell no, but here he was practically running an architecture company and he appeared to actually have his shit together.

"What are we betting on exactly?"

"Bragging rights?" He looked so relaxed sitting across from me, and for a moment, I wondered what would have happened if Tucker had never come looking for me that night.

"Lame." I rolled my eyes. "I'm competitive. I need to actually win something. Actually, let's make this interesting." I rubbed my hands together. "The first one to get laid at the wedding loses."

He grinned. "A hundred bucks."

"Fine. A hundred dollars to the loser who can't get laid."

I stuck my hand out in his direction. He gripped it firmly in his and shook, but he didn't let go.

I tried not to think about how warm his hands were or how I could feel the small calluses on his fingers from where he constantly drew with his drafting pencil.

"Deal." He smirked at me, and I got a glimpse of the old Jase. "But it really sucks winning all the time."

"We'll see about that." I dropped his hand and took a long drink of my beer. "Now get out of my office. I have work to do."

CHAPTER 7
SOPHIE

Walking into work the next morning, I felt lighter than I had in a while. Tom looked shocked when I laid the correctly formatted report in front of him during our team meeting. I didn't care if he knew that I had to get help from Jase to get it right. All that mattered was that he kept his mouth shut and didn't even consider snapping at me over it.

Instead, he basically ignored the fact that I existed and continued on as if the report that he made me stay late to work on didn't even matter.

I just smiled at him and took notes as he went over the Anderson Development and our team's plans. They were simple, uncomplicated, and honestly, a bit unimpressive. When I opened my mouth to offer a suggestion, Tom handed me another paper filled with his chicken scratch and asked me to get it typed up for him. From that moment forward, I decided that I would keep my ideas to myself.

Tom droned on for a full hour before we left his office. The guys were to start designing. I was to start typing.

I swung by Jase's office to tell him thank you for his help last night, but his office door was firmly closed.

I knocked softly against the door and waited exactly two seconds before I started to walk away. I had just turned my back when his office door opened, and his head poked out.

"Sophie." His voice stopped me in my tracks.

"Hey." I could see past him into his office and I could clearly see that he had been in the middle of a meeting with two other men.

"Oh God," I whispered. "I didn't realize you were in a meeting. I'm sorry." I was such a damn idiot. A man brings me pizza one time and all the sudden I'm knocking on his door like we're best friends.

"You know." He smirked as he crossed his arms and leaned against his doorjamb like there was no one waiting for him in his office. "That's the first time I've ever heard you say you're sorry."

I looked at the men behind him who could clearly hear our conversation then back to him. "That's not true."

"Isn't it?" He cocked an eyebrow at me, and I tried to remember if either of us had ever said I'm sorry.

Now wasn't the time, but I couldn't think of anything else.

"Well, I am sorry." I looked anywhere but at him. "But I actually came by to tell you thank you for helping me last night." My gaze settled on one of the men who was now turned and watching us. I didn't know who he was, but I knew for certain that it wasn't professional for Jase and me to be talking like this in front of him.

"But this isn't important." I took a step back. "I'm sorry for interrupting you."

Jase didn't even move. "Was it how Tom wanted it?"

I shrugged my shoulders. "He didn't throw it back in my face."

He chuckled. "I'd call that success then."

"For sure." I looked toward my office. "Alright, I'll let you get back to work."

I took off in the direction of my office, but I was only a couple steps away when Jase's voice called out behind me.

"For what it's worth, I'm sorry too."

...

I overanalyzed and dissected Jase's and my conversation so many times that it was embarrassing. I thought about it while I was making my third cup of coffee for the day. I stressed about it while I scrubbed myself with my loofa in the shower. And as badly as I didn't want to admit it, I even Googled the definition of sorry after I had tossed and turned in bed for forty-five minutes with no trace of sleep.

We hadn't said that we were sorry in five years.

Five fucking years.

Now all of a sudden we both had a conscience and were pouring out our feelings.

I blamed it on the pizza. He knew what he was doing when he ordered pizza and got my favorite topping. Softening me up. He charmed me like one of his girls and I fell for it.

I was twenty-three years old. I wasn't supposed to be falling for anything related to Jase Hale anymore. I made that promise to myself a long time ago.

Ignore him. That was my plan from here on out. Or avoid him I guess I should say. I couldn't exactly ignore my boss, but I could skirt around him like he had the plague.

He made it easy for me. He wasn't at work the rest of the week. At least not that I saw. Not that I checked his door any time I was within viewing distance. That definitely wasn't happening.

I also didn't stalk his Instagram to see that he hadn't posted a single photo in four weeks which gave me zero clue as to where he was.

"Hey, Annie." I was such an idiot.

"Hey, Sophie." She looked up from her computer to look at me. "You heading out?"

"Yeah." I smiled down at her and lifted my bag higher on my shoulder. "I have my final bridesmaid dress fitting for my brother's wedding today."

Annie's smile became bigger. "How fun!"

"For sure." I pasted on a fake smile. Getting accidentally pricked with a pin would not be fun. "I was going to try to catch Jase before I left. Is he in?"

"No." She shook her head. "He hasn't been in the office most of the week."

"Oh." I acted shocked. "I hadn't noticed." I was lying and Annie and I both knew it.

She smiled, deep and conniving. "He's been at meetings with the Anderson Development team all week. He should be back Monday though."

"Great. I'll catch him then." I shifted on my feet. I was the worst liar in the world. "Have a great weekend."

"You too, hon!"

I quickly walked out of the office before Annie could interrogate me about what I wanted to talk to Jase about. I would have cracked.

I pulled up to the seamstress and smiled at my mom who was standing outside the front door waving at me. She had been in wedding-planning mode ever since Tucker told her that he was getting married, and I would never tell her this, but her level of excitement scared me just a little bit.

"Are you ready?" she asked before I could even get fully out of the car.

"Hey, Sophie. How was work? Oh. It was great. Thank you for asking, Mom."

She rolled her eyes at my one-sided dialogue and locked arms with me.

"Just imagine." She waved toward the shop. "One day we'll be here picking out your wedding dress."

I tried to detach myself from her, but she was having none of that.

"I wouldn't hold your breath for that."

"Then get your tush in here and let me watch them dress you up as a bridesmaid. You better pretend like you're enjoying it too."

I saluted her before she pulled me in the direction of the shop.

Mrs. Maples squealed as we walked in the door and cupped my cheek in her hand. She turned me this way and that to get a good look at me before telling me how beautiful I was becoming. Mr. and Mrs. Maples owned the shop that contained wedding dresses, suits, and bridesmaids dresses in about every single color you could possibly imagine. They also carried formal dresses for homecomings and proms, and my mother and I had been coming here for such dresses since my freshman year of high school.

She and my mother gabbed about me, the wedding, and all sorts of gossip about people in our town before she finally went toward the back to grab dresses for both me and my mom.

I let my mom go first.

She had picked out a light pink dress that went to the ground but showed a hint of cleavage.

"Ay Mami," I called out through the shop as I leaned back in a chair in front of the mirrors.

"Hush," my mom whispered, but Mrs. Maples smiled.

"I can't hush." I fanned myself with my hand. "My momma is *fine*."

My mom rolled her eyes and straightened out the perfectly straight dress in front of the mirror.

"They never tell you how your adult children will act when they tell you to have kids," she said to Mrs. Maples who laughed.

"They also don't tell you that your momma's going to show up to your wedding looking like she's trying to seduce your dad." I put my hand over my mouth. "Wait. I take that back. That's gross."

My mom smirked at me. "I don't need a dress to seduce your dad."

"Oh God." I pulled my knees to my chest and rocked back and forth. "This isn't happening. This isn't happening."

"Oh, it's happening." My mother fluffed out her hair and struck a pose in the mirror.

"My parents don't have sex." I looked over at Mrs. Maples who couldn't stop laughing.

"We most certainly do."

"Nope. No. They don't." I shook my head.

My mom's phone started ringing, and I quickly grabbed it, praying that it wasn't my dad. When I saw Kennedy's picture pop up, I hit answer and watched as her face filled the screen.

"Sophie!" She was beaming.

"Hey, Kennedy." I waved through the little screen of the phone.

"Do you have your dress on yet?"

"Not yet. We've been busy talking about my parents' sex life."

"Sophie!"

I looked up at my mom with a smile as my brother's voice rang through the phone even though I couldn't see him. "Eww."

"Thank you!"

Kennedy smiled past the phone, and I knew she was looking up at my brother.

"She is in her dress though. Want to see?" I stood up and moved toward my mother.

"Of course!"

"Prepare yourself, girl. My mom is coming to break hearts."

My mom huffed and put her hands on her hips, but I could see the small smile that she was trying her best to hide. I turned the phone toward my mom and heard Kennedy's inhale of breath.

"Oh my God, Jojo. You look gorgeous."

"Oh." My mom waved her hand to dismiss the compliment. "Thank you."

"Tucker, come look at your mom."

There was a rustling on the other end of the phone then a loud, "Mamma mia!"

My mom's hands went right back to her hips and her eyes met mine. "I swear you two are just alike."

I laughed and handed the phone over to my mom.

Mrs. Maples had my dress ready in the next changing room,

and I knew that Kennedy would want to see it. Luckily, Kennedy was a wonderful bride and had picked out bridesmaids dresses that were flattering and the lightest shade of pink.

I slipped the dress over my head and called out for Mrs. Maples to zip me up. The dress showed far more cleavage than my mom's with a sweetheart neckline, but it fit my body like a glove. The soft fabric fell to the floor and showed a bit of leg from the slits on the side.

I stepped out of the dressing room and shimmied my chest toward my mom. "There's going to be a few Moore women breaking hearts at this wedding."

It all happened at once after that.

My mom snorted, Kennedy's squeal rang out through the phone, Mr. Maples looked away so quickly you would have thought I was naked, and my gaze crashed into Jase's as I almost tripped over my own feet.

No. No. No.

Jase was standing next to my mom, and even though I knew he didn't, I prayed he somehow missed my tits bouncing around in my dress like a drunk sorority girl at Mardi Gras.

"Good. Maybe one of you all will finally have me a grandbaby." My mother winked at Kennedy through the phone.

"Oh God." The words were barely a whisper out of my mouth.

"Take it down a notch, Mom," my brother yelled.

"Jase. What about you?" My mom turned back in his direction, but he was still staring at me.

"Not happening any time soon."

"I don't know." Kennedy giggled. "That suit is looking

pretty hot." She wagged her eyebrows in Jase's direction. "Ow. Don't pinch me, Tucker."

"You do look handsome, Jase." My mom straightened the label of his jacket with the hand that wasn't holding the phone. "Doesn't he, Soph?"

"What?" I looked away from him to look at my mom. "Oh. Of course. Yes. He does."

Jase grinned, and I regretted everything I had just said.

My mom went back to the pedestal in front of the mirror and started pointing out something to Mrs. Maples. I stared in her direction and tried to pretend that Jase wasn't standing right there looking like a full damn meal while I was starving.

He moved, and I held my breath as he slowly came up behind me. "You look gorgeous." His voice was soft and only for me.

"Thank you." I still didn't turn to look at him.

I jumped, my skin on fire, as he lifted a finger and pushed my hair behind my shoulder. I looked in the mirror in front of my mom and caught a glimpse of us. Jase and I. We looked good together. We looked like we belonged, but I knew that was a trick.

"You're going to lose this bet." His breath kissed my skin and goose bumps pebbled on my skin.

"I don't think so." I finally looked over my shoulder and let my gaze run over him from head to toe.

He really did look fucking handsome. It was almost unfair how good he looked.

"You always were a sore loser." He smiled, and his gaze dropped to my breasts.

"I won't be sore after this wedding." His gaze jumped back up to mine. "Not from losing or from fucking."

He opened his mouth to say something, and God, I was dying to know what he was going to say, but my mother interrupted him.

"Jase, why don't you come to our house for dinner tonight?"

I took the opportunity to move away from him and got up on the pedestal so Mrs. Maples could take a look over my dress.

"I don't want to intrude." Jase put his hands in his pockets.

"Nonsense. I'm not taking no for an answer." She looked up at me through the mirror and smiled. "It will be just like old times."

CHAPTER 8
SOPHIE

I felt like I was in high school all over again.

Jase Hale was coming to my house, and he wasn't coming there for me.

My mom knew that Jase and I hadn't had the greatest relationship in some time. She also knew that he was my new boss. She didn't care about either. When I asked her to call him and tell him that she had to cancel, you would have thought I'd asked her not to put any sugar in our iced tea.

Southern hospitality sin.

You don't invite someone over then cancel your plans, and you sure as hell didn't drink tea that wasn't sweet.

My mom's exact terms were to *suck it up*. Apparently Southern hospitality didn't apply to your children.

I was stirring more butter into the mashed potatoes when the doorbell rang, and I listened as my mom scolded Jase for ringing the doorbell in the first place. I'm pretty sure it was the first time he had ever used it.

I kept myself busy stirring mashed potatoes until every trace of butter was gone from sight then taste-tested the macaroni and cheese for quality control. My parents were both in the living room with Jase, and I could hear the three of them talk as my dad pounded Jase with questions about work and life in general.

When my mom finally walked back into the kitchen, I was sure my mouth had a solid ring of cheese around it.

"Are you going to help me put everything on the table or are you going to just keep eating?" She looked at me like I had lost my mind.

I attempted to swallow around all the cheesy goodness but still managed to answer her with my mouth full. "Both."

She rolled her eyes and carried a tray of pork chops out to the dining room table. I followed her with the bowl of macaroni and cheese I had been hovering over and the mashed potatoes. Once the table was all set, she called for my dad and Jase like it was the most normal thing to have him at our house.

I guess it was, but that was before we were working together.

Jase smiled at me as he came into the dining room with my dad. I returned it with one of my own and prayed that my teeth weren't covered in cheese.

"Sophie." He had his hands in his pockets, and for a second, I wondered if he felt as awkward about this as I did.

"Hey, Jase." I pulled out my chair and took a seat at the table.

"Jase was telling me how good a job you're doing, Soph." My dad grabbed the mashed potatoes and spooned a helping on his plate.

"Did he now?" I cocked an eyebrow in Jase's direction.

"In fairness." Jase took the macaroni my mom was

handing to him and served himself. "I didn't tell him about your drinking on the job."

My mouth popped open and I almost dropped the pork chop I had just lifted off the tray.

"Sophie Anne." My mom's voice was pure shock. "How dare you?"

I sputtered and stared at the giant smirk on Jase's face. "Jase is the one who gave it to me."

"Don't you blame him, young lady." Jase snorted, and my mom's attention turned to him. "Why did you give my daughter alcohol?"

Jase straightened in his chair, and I smirked that the tables were now turned on him. "Technically, I gave her food and alcohol. She was having a hard day."

"Well, that was sweet."

My mom believed him. Technically what he was saying was true, but he was still full of shit.

"Technically, it was also way after office hours." I was cutting through my pork chop so hard that I was surprised I didn't crack the plate. "Plus, I tried to tell Jase no. He peer-pressured me."

"Alright, you two. That's enough." My father chuckled. "I don't know how you two manage to work together."

"We actually don't work together too often. Jase is a bigwig, you know. I'm just the coffee girl."

Jase rolled his eyes.

"I doubt that office in Seattle would have been any better," my mom said absently as she ate. "It's probably a good thing you didn't hear back from them."

Jase looked up at me, but I avoided his gaze. We didn't talk about me applying for any other jobs before I took the position at Norman Architecture, but I figured he'd gotten the picture when my brother called begging on my behalf. I didn't plan on talking about it with him tonight either.

My dad asked Jase something and all talk of Seattle was forgotten.

We were almost at the home stretch. I was stuffing my last bite of mashed potatoes in my mouth, and I could hear my bed calling my name from the dining room table when my mom had to go and open her big mouth again.

"Sophie, why don't you show Jase your little apartment."

Mashed potatoes almost brought me to my death. I choked on the buttery goodness and coughed into my napkin. My mom continued like she barely even noticed.

"Jase, I think you'll be impressed with what Arnie did with the space."

"Of course." Jase smiled at my mom then looked over at me and my public display of awkwardness. "I don't want Sophie to pass out over it though."

My mom patted my back and waved off his concern.

"You know Sophie's always had a little crush on you. She'll be fine."

I held up my hand to cut them all off and took a deep breath.

"I am not ten anymore. I do not have a crush on Jase."

My mom lifted her napkin to block her mouth from my view. "Or thirteen or sixteen or eighteen."

"I swear to God." I stood up from my chair. "Come on, Jase. Let's go see my apartment."

Which I didn't clean.

It didn't matter though. I would let him take a tour of my panty drawer if it meant I could get him away from my crazy mom.

Jase thanked my parents for dinner and gabbed to my

mom about how her cooking had only gotten better over time before he finally followed me out the back door toward the garage.

"You don't have to show me your apartment." He was grinning, and I knew that he was getting a kick out of my discomfort.

"It's fine." I pulled open the door and started up the stairs with him on my tail.

We stepped into my apartment, and I thanked God that I had at least thrown away the Chinese takeout leftovers.

"This is nice." He moved around the living room which basically doubled as my bedroom. It was basically like one big loft with a small living room area, bedroom, kitchenette, and bathroom.

"Yeah. Dad did a good job." I looked in the kitchen and almost tripped over my feet as I ran toward the bras and panties I had hand-washed earlier that were now hanging off every cabinet handle to dry.

Jase stepped into my path before I could get there and lifted a pair of black lace thongs with one finger. "He has an interesting taste in decorations though."

I snatched my panties off his finger before frantically grabbing the rest of my delicates off each handle and holding them against my chest. "It was laundry day."

Jase smiled, and I ignored the way it made my chest feel tight. Instead, I focused on stuffing all of my unmentionables into a drawer. Yes. It was the silverware drawer, but I would deal with that later.

Jase cocked his head to the side and raised an eyebrow.

"Over here is the bedroom." I waved my hand in that direction and tried to lead him away from the scene of the panty crime.

"Is this where all the magic happens?" He wagged his eyebrows.

"Oh yeah." I sat down on the edge of the bed. "If by magic you mean sleep and reading and watching too much Netflix, this place is pretty damn magical." I patted my mattress.

Jase laughed and grabbed something off the top of my dresser. "And drawing?" He held up the plans I had been working on for the Anderson Development.

There was something about him seeing those drawings that embarrassed me far more than my panties ever could.

"That's nothing." I tried to grab them out of his hands, but he moved them out of my reach.

"These are good." He flipped through the rough sketches. "Really good."

I reached out for them again, but he turned to block my attempt.

"Give them to me, Jase."

He didn't. He just kept his back turned to me and continued to block me as I grabbed for my damn sketches.

Finally, once he had looked his fill, he held them out to me.

I growled at him, actually growled, and jerked them out of his hands.

"I'm not kidding, Sophie. Those are really good. You should show them to Tom."

I laughed, a big obnoxious laugh then stuffed those sketches in a drawer where they didn't belong just like my panties. "Not happening."

"You always were such a brat."

My mouth popped open. "Did you just call me a brat?" I narrowed my eyes at him.

"Yeah." He ran his hand over the short scruff on his face.

"Well, you were always an asshole." I put my hands on my hips and tried to match his stature.

"See." He pointed a finger at me. "Brat."

"I swear to God, Jase."

"What are you going to do?" He smirked, and I knew that damn smirk got him away with far too much in his life. "Threaten your boss?"

"Tom's my boss. Remember?"

"But I'm Tom's boss." He looked so smug and the urge to kiss that damn look off his face was overwhelming.

He moved an inch closer to me, and if I didn't know better, I could have sworn he was staring at my mouth.

I held my breath as I waited to see what he'd do. I wanted to push him away, but my body was begging him to move closer. My breath rushed out, and no matter how much I tried, I couldn't talk my heart into slowing down. I licked my dry lips and his gaze jumped up to mine.

He looked as confused as I felt, but he managed to take a step back.

"Goodnight, Sophie." His gaze jumped back to my lips for only a second before his face turned hard as stone. He didn't utter another word as he turned on his heel and left my apartment.

"Goodnight," I whispered to the empty room.

CHAPTER 9
SOPHIE

I thought I had put my years of confusion over Jase behind me, but it seemed like those years were just teasers. Adult Jase blew my teenage hormones out of the water. He was more confusing than ever.

I sat at my desk and pecked my fingers against the keyboard. Focusing on work was impossible. Not that Tom had actually given me much to do anyway. He wanted me to research developments similar to what we were to design.

So, Google and I were staring at each other. Google was as confused on what I was looking for as I was.

A soft knock on my door made me look up from my screen, and I startled a bit when I saw Jase standing there.

"Hey." I fiddled with the papers on my desk even though they were already in perfect order.

"You busy?" He ran his hand over the back of his head, and it was the first time since we were kids that I had seen him look a bit nervous.

"Just doing some research for Tom." I shrugged my shoulders.

"Good. Come on." He nodded his head toward the door.

I didn't move an inch. "Where are we going?"

"Grab your purse." Then he walked out leaving me clueless behind him.

But this time I did what he said.

I followed him as he led me out the front door. I waved to Annie, and she waved back with a giant smile on her face.

Jase walked up to a shiny new SUV that looked like it cost more money than I've had in my entire lifetime. I let out a low whistle. "You fancy, huh?"

He rolled his eyes at me. "Get in."

I opened the door and climbed in as Jase clicked his seat belt in place.

He pulled out of the parking lot, and I was acutely aware of how close he was to me.

I was also extremely aware that he hadn't said a single word since we got in the car.

I started pressing buttons on the impressive screen between us even though I had no clue what I was doing, but eventually I managed to get some music to start playing through the speakers. I searched through the stations finding nothing but boring talking. I pressed the button that connected to his phone, and song after song listed on the screen from some sort of playlist.

"Sophie." Jase grabbed for my hand, but I was already pressing my finger against the screen.

Within seconds, Missy Elliott's "Work It" started blaring through the speakers and Jase let out of low groan as I started rapping.

"This is on your playlist," I reminded him over the music before getting back to my jam.

He sat there stiff as a board while I rapped and danced in

my seat. I kept catching his gaze even though he was pretending not to watch me, but then a smile broke out across his face, and I knew that I had him.

"I know you know the words, Jase. Don't let me down."

He laughed, a deep belly laugh, then his lips started moving while he started singing with Missy about getting our hair did.

It was so easy. The way we started falling back into who we were before we ruined everything.

We sang, we laughed, I danced.

Jase brushed his shoulder off like all the boys did when we were in high school and they thought they were cool.

By the time he parked the car, I was laughing hysterically, and I couldn't even remember what I was so worried about earlier. I could barely remember why I ever hated him.

He turned off the car and Missy disappeared along with the hum of the engine.

"I can't believe you're a closet Missy Elliott lover." I leaned my head back against the headrest.

"I am not a closet Missy Elliott lover." He held up one finger. "Name one person who doesn't love that song."

"Hey." I held up my hands in surrender. "I'm not judging. That's my jam. I just didn't realize it was also your jam."

"Whatever." He nudged his elbow against mine on the armrest. "Let's go."

"Are you taking me to lunch?" I looked out the windshield at the restaurant in front of us. "I know we just made strides in bonding, but I didn't know we were here yet."

"Your boss is here." He opened the door and stood.

"Tom?" I shrieked. Eating lunch with Tom wasn't on the top of my to-do list. Being around him as little as possible? That was number one.

"No." He shoved his keys in his pocket.

I still hadn't even unbuckled.

"Mr. Norman." He closed the door and I scrambled to get out of his SUV and catch up with him.

"Mr. Norman?" I whispered as I walk/ran behind him. "As in the owner of Norman Architecture, Mr. Norman?"

"That would be the one." He smiled at me over his shoulder.

"Why didn't you warn me?" I straightened out my skirt. "I would have dressed better."

"You look gorgeous." He said it absently, but it didn't matter. It still made my stomach flutter.

"I look like I've been at a Missy Elliott concert." I looked into a window as we passed and tried to tame my flyaways that got a mind of their own during our little dance party.

Jase opened the door and motioned for me to go in before him. I did but looked back at him hesitantly over my shoulder.

I wasn't prepared to meet our boss.

Not physically or mentally.

I was going to tell him that, but his eyes were firmly planted on my ass.

I snapped my fingers. "Up here, Mr. Hale."

He smirked, not even trying to hide the fact that he was checking out my ass.

"Sorry."

He didn't look an ounce sorry.

As soon as we walked in, Jase held up his hand and waved at someone toward the back of the restaurant. I couldn't see them so I followed behind Jase as he led the way.

There was a man and a woman sitting at the table. Both

of them looked to be in their late sixties, and I instantly recognized the man from Jase's office the day I interrupted his meeting.

He stood as soon as we made it to the table.

"Sophie, this is Mr. and Mrs. Norman," Jase said before looking toward them. "This is Sophie Moore."

Mr. Norman held out his hand toward me and I took it. "I'm Dan." He rolled his eyes toward Jase who was hugging Mrs. Norman. "I keep telling him to quit calling me Mr. Norman, but he doesn't listen to a damn thing I say."

And just like that, I felt ten times more at ease.

"It's nice to meet you, Dan."

Mrs. Norman made her way around the table to us, and she ignored the hand I held out in her direction and pulled me into a hug.

"I'm Erin." She pulled back a tiny bit and really looked at me with a gentle smile on her face.

Jase pulled my chair out for me as we sat down, and my cheeks heated as Erin watched him. It was an innocent move, but it felt like more with her seeing it.

"So, Sophie." Dan pulled his napkin into his lap. "Jase tells me you're already doing amazing."

"I don't know about that." I laughed and looked over at Jase who was looking down at his menu. "I'm just trying to do whatever Tom tells me."

Dan chuckled, but Erin scoffed.

"I don't know why you all don't just fire that old jerk." She looked back and forth between her husband and Jase.

"He's not been that bad," I lied.

"You're sweet." Erin turned her attention toward me. "But that man has worked for my husband going on twenty years, and he's always been an asshole."

"But he's a smart asshole." Dan shrugged his shoulders.

"That's what I told her." Jase set his menu down in front of him. "She could learn a lot from him."

"You're not the one getting him coffee every day," I mumbled.

"He was." Dan tapped his finger on the table. "How long were you under Tom for?"

I looked over at Jase. He didn't tell me that he had worked under Tom, just that he had been in my position. Sure, he had given me the draft for that report, but I had no idea he had because he had been where I now stood.

"Two years." He rubbed at the back of his neck. "A very long two years."

"I didn't know that."

"It's a time I like to forget."

I laughed, but I doubted he was lying.

"So, Sophie." Erin put her elbows on the table and leaned closer to me. "I'm not used to having many women around except for Annie. We should get together sometime so you can give me all the office gossip without these two."

"For sure." I hiked my thumb toward Jase. "I have so much dirt on Jase that you could blackmail him for years."

"Oh good." She rubbed her hands together. "I can't get anything out of Annie. She coddles these two too much."

I nodded my head because I one hundred percent agreed with her. At least when it came to Jase. "Did you know that she bakes treats for company meetings, but she always holds some back for Jase so he doesn't have to fight the masses?"

"That's ridiculous." She rolled her eyes at a smirking Jase.

"I know. I mean, fight for your brownies if you want them. Build some character."

Dan started coughing as he almost choked on his water.

"You think I need to build character?" Jase knocked his elbow into mine.

"Everyone needs to build character. Don't be so sensitive."

Jase scoffed and looked at Erin. "I have loads of dirt on Sophie too."

"He doesn't." I shook my head.

"I do." He turned toward me. "On the way over here, she made me"—he pointed to his chest—"her boss, listen to very inappropriate music."

My mouth popped open and I narrowed my eyes at him.

"What song?" Dan asked with a chuckle.

"'Work It' by Missy Elliott." Jase crossed his arms as if he had just told them I was doing a bit of prostituting on the side.

"No way." Erin slapped her hand against the table. "That's my jam."

I looked up at Erin with her light blond hair that was sprinkled with grey and I couldn't help but smile.

Then I kicked Jase under the table like the brat that he accused me of being and said, "It's Jase's too."

CHAPTER 10
JASE

I was completely off my game.

I couldn't concentrate on work, I couldn't manage to care about the emails I needed to return, and I sure as hell couldn't think about anything other than Sophie.

She was fucking with my head.

Taking her to lunch yesterday was a bad idea. She was charming and gorgeous, and Mr. Norman was eating out of the palm of her hand by the time they finally handed me the bill. I didn't blame him though. I was right there with him.

Which was why I stayed away from the office today. I had meeting after meeting with the executives for the Anderson Development, but I decided to work from home after. I never worked from home. I couldn't seem to get shit done here.

But it was better than being near her.

Or so I thought.

I clicked on my phone and scrolled through the names. I needed to get laid. It had been far too long, and sexual frustration wasn't helping my situation.

My cock was in my hand more nights than it wasn't, and since Sophie started working at my office, she had become the star of the show most nights.

I sent a message to Grace. I hadn't talked to her in quite some time, but she was eager, to say the least. And according to Annie, she had still been leaving messages for me at the office.

My phone chimed within minutes of me sending my message. "I'd love to go to dinner."

After jumping in the shower and washing away the day, I threw on a pair of jeans and a white t-shirt. We weren't going anywhere fancy. I didn't want to give her the wrong impression.

I knew that made me a dick, but honestly, I didn't really care at that moment.

Grace wrapped her arm in mine as the hostess took us to our table. She had been subtly touching me since the moment I picked her up at her apartment. She was wearing a dress that was probably a bit too short, but it looked amazing on her ass.

Or her ass looked amazing in it. However you want to look at it.

All I knew was that looking at her ass should have made me feel better. What it shouldn't do was make me think about Sophie and how her ass looked amazing in anything.

She didn't need a short dress for me to admire it. But now I couldn't stop thinking about what her ass would look like in that dress.

"Are you okay?"

I looked up at Grace and told myself to stop thinking about Sophie's ass.

"I'm fine." I pointed down to the menu. "Just trying to figure out what I want."

That was the understatement of the century.

"I usually get the blackened chicken salad from here. It's really good."

Of course, she did.

I nodded my head like I was actually interested in some fucking salad. I just wanted to get this dinner over with and get to the house.

The server came to the table and Grace ordered the salad and I ordered a steak.

"It was good to finally hear from you again." She shifted in her seat. "I was worried that you lost my number."

I leaned back in my chair and looked at her. She was beautiful. So fucking beautiful, but it somehow didn't matter to me today.

And that pissed me off.

"I've been really busy with work." It wasn't a lie, but it also wasn't the whole truth. "This is actually one of the first evenings I've had off."

"And you decided to spend it with me?" There was a sparkle in her eyes as she said the words that made me sit up a little straighter.

"It looks like I did."

I had been upfront with Grace since the first time I met her. I wasn't looking for a relationship. My only girlfriend was my job, and I wanted to keep it that way. She had been cool with it then, but there was always that inevitable moment when being cool with it changed. It always did.

After tonight, I wouldn't be able to call her again. Not without having that damn conversation on repeat.

She continued to talk about everything under the sun.

Half the time she didn't really mind whether I responded or not. She just kept going. I was worried that the evening would be completely lost until she took a sip of her water and asked, "Are we going back to your place tonight or are you coming to mine?"

"Yours." I held up my hand to grab the waiter's attention and handed him my debit card before he could show me the check.

I was ready to get out of this damn place.

He brought back my card, and I quickly signed the receipt before helping Grace out of her chair.

It didn't slip my mind that I had more fun at lunch yesterday with Sophie and our boss than I did on a date tonight with Grace, but it wasn't like I was expecting anything different. Grace was fun in the bedroom, and that was all that mattered at the moment.

Grace pressed against my side and wrapped her arm around mine as we made our way out of the restaurant. I rubbed my nose as the smell of her perfume overwhelmed me.

We were almost there, the door in view when laughter to my right drew my attention and my gaze landed on Sophie. I couldn't get a good look at the person who was sitting across from her, but the idea that it might be a man made my blood boil.

I hated that my heart was racing as I led Grace toward her table.

I hated that Grace smiled at me like I was going to introduce her to someone I knew because she was important to me.

I hated that I couldn't bring myself to leave without seeing who Sophie was with.

"Hey, Soph." I called her the nickname that I hadn't said out loud in years.

She blinked up at me and wrinkled her brow. "Hey."

I stood there awkwardly for a moment while I thought about what the hell to say. This wasn't like me. I was smooth. I was charming. I wasn't the guy who made a fool out of himself because his new employee was out with another girl.

I was such an idiot.

What did it matter if she was with some other guy?

Some other guy? Like she was supposed to be with me.

I didn't want to date Sophie Moore.

I just didn't like the idea of her dating anyone else either.

I was a selfish bastard. I knew it and so did she. It was why she had spent so many years hating me.

"How are you?" I started to put my hands in my pockets, but Grace's arm wrapped around mine blocked my path. Sophie's attention snapped to that exact spot with the movement.

"I'm fine. You?" She was still staring at Grace's arm touching mine, and I wished she would look up at me.

"I'm sorry." I shook my head. "This is Grace. Grace, this is Sophie."

"It's nice to meet you." Grace smiled at Sophie, but Sophie's returning one was much more forced.

"You too." She didn't introduce her friend, so I pulled my arm out of Grace's and held my hand out in her direction.

"I'm Jase."

She quickly wiped her hand on her napkin then shook my hand.

"Jodie."

Sophie was looking down at her dinner like it had

offended her, and I couldn't catch her gaze again no matter how hard I tried.

The urge to tell her that Grace meant nothing to me was overwhelming. I didn't owe her an explanation. She was my best friend's sister and my employee. My fucking employee. I needed to remember that.

None of that made a difference.

"I'll see you tomorrow at work." I tucked my free hand in my pocket to stop myself from reaching out to her. It didn't matter that Grace was clinging to me like I was her long-lost love. I needed to do something.

Everything about Grace felt wrong.

If I hadn't felt that way before, Sophie's face when she looked up at me made me itch to pull away from Grace.

"I have a pretty busy day tomorrow, but maybe I'll see you around."

She was dismissing me. I knew it, she knew it, and her friend who was covering her smile with her napkin knew it.

"Alright." I forced a smile at her. "But don't work too hard."

"You either." She flippantly waved her hand in the direction of me and Grace. "From all the women you've been flaunting around, you're likely to pull a muscle or something."

Grace tensed next to me, but I grinned.

I hated that seeing me out with Grace could possibly be hurting her, but it also meant she cared.

"Don't you worry about my muscles." I patted my stomach and Sophie rolled her eyes. "They're in pretty good condition."

"That ego is too." She popped one of her French fries in her mouth.

"You two work together?" Grace asked me quietly, but Sophie heard.

"Yeah. He's my boss." She leaned closer toward Grace. "It's like every office romance fantasy come true. If you think he's good in your bed, just imagine what he can do on a desk." She fanned herself dramatically.

"Alright, Sophie." I looked over at Grace, but she was now looking anywhere but at me. "I'll see you tomorrow."

She waved at me with a sparkle in her eyes. "I can't wait."

Grace and I walked out of the restaurant still arm and arm even though she was barely touching me now.

I should be pissed.

Sophie probably just ruined every chance I had for tonight, but I couldn't bring myself to care.

Her laughter trailed behind us, and I couldn't stop smiling.

...

Grace was pissed.

Apparently, she didn't find Sophie funny or cute or charming as hell.

Trust me.

She bitched about her almost the entire way to her apartment. Every word grated on my nerves. Sure, Sophie was a bit out of line, but she obviously wasn't serious. Grace didn't care.

When we made it to her apartment, I was surprised when she still invited me inside. I stood outside her door, and I told myself to get it together. I needed to get laid. That fact couldn't be argued, but I couldn't stand it when her hand trailed down my arm.

It felt wrong.

Completely wrong.

"I think I better head home." I slowly pulled my hand away from hers. "I have to be at the office early tomorrow."

Her eyes hardened. "With Sophie?"

"No." I shook my head. "Not with Sophie. With my job."

She crossed her arms and turned her head slightly away from me.

"I don't owe you an explanation." And it pissed me off that I was giving her one. "But I've never fucked anyone in my office. Sophie was just being a brat."

"Then take me to your office." She batted her lashes at me, and I could have.

I could take her to my office, bend her over my desk, and try my hardest to fuck Sophie right out of my head.

If it had been two weeks ago, I would have. Without a second thought.

But I couldn't.

That was the most fucked-up part.

"Not tonight," I said softly, but her face fell just the same.

She pushed her keys into her front door and hesitated for only a second. "Do me a favor, Jase. Lose my number for real this time."

CHAPTER 11
SOPHIE

"This isn't right." Tom threw the report back across his desk toward me. "You've got your numbers mixed up somehow."

I opened my mouth to argue, but he was right. I had fucked them up.

"I'm sorry." I flipped through the pages. "I'll fix it."

Tom shook his head as if he was beyond irritated with me. "I need them tomorrow so make sure they are right this time."

"Of course." I could feel my face heating as I walked out of his office. I didn't know what the hell was wrong with me. I spilled coffee on my shirt this morning and had been rocking that stain all day, I forgot to hit save on something I had been working on earlier and had to do the whole thing over again, and now this.

I blamed it on lack of sleep and hormones.

I was just getting off my period and a woman had to have a grace period to get her hormones back in check before she was expected to act like a normal human again.

It had absolutely nothing to do with Jase. I didn't toss and turn in bed last night obsessing over what he was probably doing with that girl.

What was her name? Grace. Don't let me fool you. I knew her name. I had looked her up on Facebook as soon as I had gotten home. I needed the privacy to bring out my inner stalker that all of us women had hiding somewhere inside of us.

Some a little more than others.

Mine was simply for research purposes.

Maybe Jase was planning on bringing her as his date to my brother's wedding in a couple weeks. I would either have to avoid her or apologize for what I said about being on Jase's desk, but hopefully she had a sense of humor.

According to her Instagram, all she had was a sense of how hot she was. It was picture after picture of her in almost no clothes posing for the camera. It was easy to see why Jase went out with her.

I was even tempted to hit that little follow button so I could look at her every day, but everyone knew that Stalker 101 meant never hitting that follow button.

That would be Defcon 1.

Instead, I turned off my phone and tried my hardest not to think about either of them. I didn't imagine what he was doing at that exact moment. I didn't try to remember what his hands had felt like on my own body, as if I could forget.

It was too much.

I knew that Jase slept around. I wasn't an idiot, but there was something about seeing the girl, about knowing who he was with, that completely fucked with my head.

I wasn't an idiot.

I knew who Jase was, and I knew that no matter how

well we were getting along at work, that was all it would ever be.

Jase was a heartbreaker through and through.

I had been on the receiving end of it before, and I had absolutely no plans to be there again.

But I couldn't get my head, my heart, and my body all on the same page. Which meant I would be staying late at work *again*. I take back what I said earlier. This is all Jase's fault.

It was his fault that I had no sleep, it was his fault that my head wasn't where it needed to be, and it was most certainly his fault that I was having the mixed urge to punch him or kiss him.

All while he was with her.

Hating Jase Hale was far easier than liking him, and I needed to remember that.

I was at Norman Architecture for two reasons: a paycheck and a career. Nothing outside of those two things mattered. It didn't matter that Tom was an asshole or that my non-relationship with Jase was the most confusing thing to ever happen to me.

Do my job. Get paid. Go home. It was that easy.

After that I could worry about things like moving out of my parents' house, getting a car that wasn't fifteen years old, and maybe finding someone to date.

But I wasn't in a position for any of those things.

My bank account had fewer commas than a high schooler's Facebook post, and my list of prospective dates was even smaller.

So, putting my head down, forgetting about Jase Hale, and redoing this report that I never should have messed up were my only priorities.

I didn't have time to worry about anything else.

Sticking to my plan would be easy. A piece of cake.

Except I forgot about one small little detail. Forgetting Jase when he was still my boss was practically impossible. Especially when he came into my office and took a seat on the edge of my desk like he owned the place.

I continued typing my report and refused to look up at him.

I had managed to avoid him around the office all day today, and yet, here he was.

"Are you avoiding me?" He picked up a pen off my desk and twirled it between his fingers.

"Nope." I turned the page on my report and kept typing.

"Are you sure?" He was teasing me, but I wasn't in the mood.

"Do you need something?" I looked up at him. "I'm busy and would love to leave the office before midnight."

He jerked back a little at my tone and an apology sat on the tip of my tongue.

"Are you mad?" He leaned farther on my desk and I wanted to smack him as he laid his hand across the report I was currently working on.

"No. I'm not mad." I jerked the paper out from under his hand. "Why would I be mad?"

"I don't know." He looked like he was truly confused. "I know this can't be about last night. You're the one who told my date I was fucking girls at the office. I should be pissed at you."

"Oh please." I rolled my eyes and tried to squash the tightness in my chest. "If she ever came to the office, she'd know that your only options are Annie, me, and some girl who works in Interior Design. Pickings are slim."

He grinned, and I swear that man's smile could get him any woman he wanted.

"I don't know." He ran his hand over his jaw. "Haley in Interior Design is kind of hot."

I forced a smile while gritting my teeth. "Get out, Jase."

He didn't move an inch. "I'm kidding." His gaze searched my face. "You remember jokes? You had them last night."

"And you had far more than that." I stood from my chair and moved toward the door to show him out.

Jase turned to face me. He was still sitting on the edge of my desk, and his legs were stretched out and crossed in front of him as if he had no intention of leaving any time soon.

"Sophie Moore, are you jealous?"

"Be serious." His words rang right through me. "I have no interest in being one of your one-night stands."

"You did once upon a time." He grinned as I narrowed my eyes. "If my memory serves me correct, you were practically begging for it."

"Fuck you." I stormed closer to him. "Nobody made you do anything you didn't want to do. Even if you regretted it after."

"You think I regretted it?" He stood to his full height and I felt even more overwhelmed than just a moment before.

"Of course you did. What was I supposed to think? You ran from my brother."

"He's my best friend," he growled at me, and I was suddenly aware that we were still in my office.

"Be quiet." I quickly shut the door in case anyone else was still in the office. I didn't need our laundry aired throughout the whole damn place.

"Don't tell me to be quiet." He ran his hand through his hair and took a step closer to me. We were only about a foot away from each other, but it felt like a mile. He was too close yet so far away. "You don't get to decide how I felt in that moment. I was so overwhelmed because I had been dreaming of touching you for as long as I could remember, and I was scared to death that your brother was going to hate me."

I wouldn't let his words affect me. "You didn't dream of touching me."

"Do you know how many times I've had my cock in my hand while I thought about you? Do you have any idea how many times I imagined you on your knees in front of me with my cock between your lips?"

My thighs tightened involuntarily.

"Your brother has been the closest thing to family I've ever had. I didn't want to lose him."

He had moved even closer to me, and I couldn't stop watching the rapid rise and fall of his chest.

"And now?" My words were barely a whisper.

"Now." My gaze jumped up to meet his. "I can't seem to care about any repercussions."

His hand fisted in my hair so quickly that I didn't have time to do anything other than open my mouth to him on a moan. His mouth devoured mine. The smooth Jase that I had known all my life was gone, and he was replaced with lips and teeth and a desperation I could taste on my tongue.

He took out his anger and hunger against my skin, and I clung to him desperately as I tried to draw out my own hurt against his neck.

He lifted me in his arms and I slammed my mouth back

against his. I didn't care where he was taking me. All that mattered was this. All I needed was him.

My ass hit my desk and I barely registered the sounds of things clattering to the ground. Jase's lips moved along my jaw, his teeth nipped at my ear, and I leaned back on my hands as he continued lower. His fingers found the buttons of my shirt and opened them with expert precision. I didn't let myself dwell on the fact that he was so much more experienced than the first time he had his hands on me because I was too.

He pulled my shirt open and his gaze feasted on my breasts. He didn't waste any time as he jerked my bra down just enough to expose me to him fully. His tongue pressed against my nipple a moment before he blew out a gentle breath. Chill bumps broke out against my skin and my hips jolted forward against his.

He was hard. So unbelievably hard, and I was dying to feel him. I leaned forward and grabbed his belt in my hands. He tried to nudge me back to continue his work on my chest, but I refused. I had thought about what he would feel like in my hand, my mouth, inside me for far too long.

I made quick work of his belt as he peppered kisses along my collarbone, and I popped the button on his slacks with a dexterity that I didn't even realize I had. I slid my hand inside his boxers and my thighs tightened around him as his cock filled my hand.

His groan was loud and almost painful, and I tightened my hand around him as he sank his teeth into my skin.

I pushed him back with my body as I stood from my desk. He looked confused for a moment, almost irritated until I dropped to my knees in front of him.

He looked to the ceiling as I pulled him out of his pants, and I watched his throat bob as he swallowed.

He was bigger than I had imagined. I figured all that cocky swagger of his was making up for something, but I was wrong. Unless he didn't know how to use it.

I licked my lips and looked up at him. He was watching me with an intensity that made my core tighten, and I couldn't stop the moan that slipped past my lips as I pushed him past them. His hands tangled in my hair, but his gaze didn't budge from mine.

I took him in my mouth as far as I could before I swirled my tongue around the tip. His hands tightened in my hair and I did it again before I took him again fully.

His thighs shook under my hands, and I had never been so turned on by giving head in my entire life. I pressed my thighs together to try to stop the insistent ache there, but it did nothing but make me want him more.

"Touch your pussy." His voice was rough and demanding, and my gaze jerked back up to him at his command. "Do it. Touch your pussy while I fuck your pretty little mouth."

I didn't hesitate again as I pushed my hand into my dress pants and moaned around his cock as I gently pressed my finger against my clit. I was so wet, and my body was desperate for release.

Jase took control of my mouth as he pushed his fingers harder into my hair and his cock harder into my mouth. My fingers matched his speed as he fucked me, and I was at the brink of coming when his next command left his lips.

"I want to taste you."

I couldn't answer him because he was still pushing in and out of my mouth at a brutal pace, so I lifted my fingers and let him suck them between his lips. I hollowed out my cheeks at the same moment, and his cock slammed against the back of my throat while his growl of pleasure filled my office.

I whimpered as he pulled out of my mouth. He had a crazed look in his eyes like he was barely in control of himself, and I fucking loved it. He reached for my hands, helping me stand, then made quick work of removing my pants.

He bent me over my desk, my ass in the air, my panties still in place, and I took a deep breath as he gripped my ass in both hands and jerked me back toward him. He was impatient and so was I.

He pulled my panties to the side, too desperate to wait any longer, and I cried out as he ran his cock up and down my slit before slamming into me.

His hands dug into my hips and my hands clung to my desk. He was ruthless in his thrusts just as I always imagined he'd be, but he was somehow gentle and giving at the same time. He pulled me toward him, my back pressing against his chest, and he continued his pace as his fingers found my clit and his lips pressed against my shoulder.

I clenched around him and started to come before I could manage a moan, and I pushed my head back on his shoulder as I fell apart around him. His fingers slowly coaxed out my orgasm while not once missing pace of his thrusts.

My body started to sag against him, but his fingers started picking up the pace to match his body. I was shocked at how quickly my body started tightening again.

"You are so fucking beautiful." Jase whispered the words amongst kisses on my neck, and it suddenly felt like too much.

Being here with him.

We needed to stop. We weren't thinking clearly, but I knew we couldn't.

I turned my face toward him and kissed him like it might be my only chance. For all I knew, it would be. He kissed me back just as frantically, and I could barely comprehend what was going on around me as he gently slapped my clit.

I screamed, my body tensing as another orgasm wracked through my body, and my body became dead weight against him as he thrust inside of me one last time. His body shook all around me, and I couldn't bring myself to say anything as I felt him come inside of me.

We didn't use a condom.

He was my brother's best friend, he was my fucking boss, he didn't wear a condom, and I couldn't bring myself to care.

I was on birth control, and as much as I hated to admit it, I trusted him.

Jase held me against him. Our heaving breaths mingled together as we tried to bring ourselves down. I knew this was just sex, but I couldn't stop myself as I cuddled deeper against him and breathed in his scent. It was more than just his cologne. It was something that was uniquely him, and just that quick hit of it made me feel like I was the same girl who used to be crazy over him.

I allowed myself one more moment. I took him in. His warmth. His smell. The way his body molded perfectly against mine. When that moment was up, I forced myself to pull away from him.

It would be too easy, and I knew it.

Falling for Jase would be like slipping into a lovely kind of déjà vu. He was like a drug. Addictive, dangerous, and destructive. I could still taste the thrill of him on my tongue, but I knew it wouldn't last.

Jase was temporary.

A quick high. An electrifying moment.

"Don't." His voice was soft as his arms tightened around me. "Just give us another minute before you get completely lost in your head."

It was too late, but I didn't tell him that. I let him hold me if only for a moment more, and I tried to just enjoy the moment.

I had no expectations when it came to him. No unrealistic dreams of happily ever afters and white picket fences. This was sex. Plain and simple.

Really great sex.

There was no need to complicate it.

I pulled back from him just a bit and watched as he searched my face.

"I have to admit that you've proven me wrong." I pulled fully out of his arms and straightened my bra.

"How so?" He looked a bit nervous about what I would say next.

"I thought I had you pegged." I pulled my shirt over my arms and started buttoning it as he righted his slacks. "Either a small dick or bad in bed."

He scoffed. "You thought I had a small dick?"

I shrugged my shoulders. "I didn't get a good feel back in the day. But I'm happy to report that neither of those are true."

He trailed his fingers over my bare thigh, and I hated that my breath caught in my throat. "I knew we'd be good together."

He pressed his lips against mine, and it caught me off guard. My hands pressed against his chest and fisted his shirt. I didn't know if I was trying to pull him closer or push him away, but I knew I couldn't let go.

"We shouldn't do this again," I whispered against his mouth.

"Of course, we should." He nipped at my lip causing the smallest moan before he smacked my ass that was only covered in my panties. "Now get back to work."

CHAPTER 12
JASE

Fucking Sophie in her office probably wasn't my smartest idea, but God, somehow it still felt like the best idea I ever had.

I slept like a rock last night, and when I got to work this morning, I got more work done in a few hours than I had been able to accomplish in the last few days.

Sophie had said that we shouldn't do it again, but she was wrong. I could see the wheels turning in her head as soon as her orgasm quit humming through her body. She was overthinking things. She always had.

Technically, she was probably right.

I was her boss, and she was my employee. I didn't read the employee handbook word for word, but I'm pretty sure there was a full section in there that stated this was off-limits.

I wouldn't let this hurt her though. I knew she needed this job. She wouldn't have wounded her pride by asking her brother to ask me for an interview if she didn't. She probably applied to every architecture firm in the country before she applied here.

If anyone found out about us, I would take the fall. The idea of that seemed a lot more reasonable than not touching her again. It wasn't an option.

She walked into the conference room for our company meeting and I couldn't take my eyes off her. She looked like she slept last night as well. She was smiling as she talked to her team member, Sean, and even though he was looking at her like she hung the moon, I didn't care. Because her gaze met mine while he was still talking, and her cheeks blushed with a shade of pink that reminded me of her panties from last night.

I adjusted my pants so the entire company wouldn't see the chub I was getting just at the damn sight of her. We had to be ready for the Anderson Development pitch in one week. Mr. Norman would be here to help me choose the best plans to present to the client, and I didn't need my team distracted by the fact that I had wood during our meeting.

There would be too many jokes that I would never live down, and honestly, I wouldn't blame them.

I just couldn't look at Sophie for the rest of the meeting. Simple as that.

Except when she moved, and my gaze instantly jumped back to where she was standing. She was wearing a black dress today that seemed to flow around her knees.

Knees.

Sophie on her knees.

Sophie's perfect pink lips wrapped around my cock while she was on her knees.

I took a seat in my chair and crossed my legs.

This was going to be hard. Pun intended.

"Alright, everyone."

Everybody turned their attention toward me. "We have a

week until the presentations for Anderson Development. We're meeting today to make sure everyone is clear on what the client expects and to see if anyone has any questions."

A few hands shot up in the room and I answered their questions as best that I could. I tried to keep my attention on the person who was talking to me, but my eyes continuously sought out Sophie. It didn't matter if she was being quiet as a mouse.

"What if our team has more than one pitch?" one of the younger architects asked. He had only been with our company for about a year, and it was clear that his team leader wasn't on the same page with him when his attention snapped in his direction.

"If your team leader thinks that both pitches should be presented then that's fine."

He wouldn't. Not now that he had gone above him.

I answered a few more questions before everyone stood to return to their jobs. Sophie was making her way toward the door when I called out to her.

"Ms. Moore, can you meet me in my office after this?"

Several eyes turned in her direction, and by the way her eyes narrowed, I knew she was pissed that I had just called her out in front of everyone.

"Of course."

She hurried from the room, but I took my time. I didn't need anyone thinking I was eager to get to my office to see her even though I was. It wasn't any of their business.

When I made it to my office, she was leaning against the wall beside my door and she was chewing on her thumbnail. She looked nervous and adorable, and I wanted nothing more than to walk up to her and press my lips against hers.

Her eyes met mine as I pressed the code into my door to unlock it. I led her inside then shut the door behind me.

"Why would you do that?" she whisper-yelled at me.

"Ms. Moore, I have your preliminary evaluation from Tom regarding how you've been performing so far."

"Oh." Her shoulders squared at my tone.

"Please have a seat." I waved to the chair in front of my desk as I took a seat in mine.

I flipped through the evaluation that I had already read twice this morning.

"Tom has rated you pretty highly in most areas."

She looked surprised by that, and I didn't blame her.

"But he wrote a note down here that you might want to work on your attitude."

"Are you shitting me?" Her fingers started turning white from her grip on the arm on the chair.

Technically the note said that she would go far if she kept her head down and focused on her work. At the bottom written in black ink: *Too much talking and questioning.*

I had to laugh when I read it. Tom thought everyone talked too much, and if you questioned him about anything, then you were pretty much set on his shit list.

But I had never seen him give someone such high ratings in the other areas. It was a stupid evaluation anyway. Mr. Norman put it in place to keep up with how new employees were doing and where they needed extra work.

According to Tom, Sophie only needed work where her mouth was involved. If he only knew how skilled she was with that mouth, he wouldn't be worried about her at all.

"I'm sorry to say that I'm not." I flipped the paper facedown. "Now comes the part that I really hate."

I huffed and ran my fingers through my hair.

"Are you firing me?" She was practically screeching.

"What?" I looked at her like she was crazy. "Of course not. But I do have to punish you."

She crossed her arms. "This is absolutely ridiculous. What are you going to do? Put me on some sort of probation period because I don't jump when Tom tells me to?"

"I could." I pushed away from my desk. "But I had something else in mind."

"Like what?" Her attitude was coming out full force now, and for a second, I didn't blame Tom.

"Come here."

"What? No." She crossed her legs and her dress rode up her thighs the tiniest bit.

"Alright." I ran my hand over my chin. "Then I guess I'll let Tom decide how to discipline you."

I wouldn't. If I hadn't been obsessing over tasting her all morning, I wouldn't even be playing this game with her now.

"You wouldn't." She said the words as she stood and made her way toward me.

She didn't trust that I wouldn't. I could lie and say that it hurt, but I liked keeping her on her toes.

She stopped when she was about a foot away from me, and I reached out for her hand and pulled her forward until her knees hit mine.

"Well, Ms. Moore." I wrapped my hands around her hips then pressed her ass against the edge of my desk. "It looks like it's all up to me then."

I gave her a teasing smile and her tongue snaked out to wet her bottom lip.

"We are at work," she whispered as I trailed my fingers at the hem of her dress.

I brought my hand higher against the inside of her thigh,

just barely above her knee, and she opened her legs almost unnoticeably.

"We were at work last night."

She rolled her eyes but didn't argue.

"Do you want me to stop?"

She didn't answer me right away. Instead, she looked toward the door that was securely locked then back at me. She was already breathing hard with barely a touch of my fingers.

I drew small patterns against her thigh and waited for her response. I wouldn't go any further unless she wanted this. I knew she did, but I needed to hear her say it.

"Don't stop."

I pushed my hand farther into her dress and gripped the edge of her panties with one finger. She lifted her ass, just barely, and I made quick work of pulling them down her thighs.

I let her panties fall to the floor before bringing my hand back under her dress. She was already so fucking wet, and I knew that she felt as desperate for this as I did.

I stood slightly, pressing my lips against her mouth. She kissed me back with an urgency that made me feel reckless. It was a push and pull. Her tongue, my teeth. Her lips, my growl.

I pulled my mouth away from hers and kissed her neck as I pushed her back against my desk. She was staring up at me, her chest was heaving under the black fabric that hid it, and she looked so damn beautiful, that it stunned me for a moment.

I pressed my lips to the inside of her knee and her leg jerked under my touch. I sat down in my chair and gripped just behind her knees. I pulled her toward me until the edge of her ass was barely resting on the desk. She let out the tiniest squeal at the sudden movement, but that quickly changed to a moan as I nipped the inside of her thigh with my teeth.

I inched her dress higher and higher as I took my time running my lips, tongue, and teeth against her skin. When I finally exposed her pussy, her fingers were gripping the edge of my desk and her rapid breathing filled the space.

I slowly ran my tongue along her slit before sucking her clit into my mouth. Sophie's back arched off the table, and her hands flew to her mouth to try to muffle her sounds that echoed through the room.

"Shh." I said the word against her skin, and her hips lifted off the table just slightly, chasing the feel of it.

I lifted her right leg over my shoulder and pushed her left one further down my desk to give me better access. Her leg trembled in my hand as I dove into her flesh. I didn't give her time to think as I took turns flicking my tongue and sucking her into my mouth.

She loved it when I just barely used my teeth. She squirmed and forced her hips harder against my mouth.

She tangled one of her hands in my hair while the other continued to cover her mouth. She was so close, so damn close, and I ran my teeth along her clit to get her an inch closer to release before I stopped.

"What the hell are you doing?" She was panting, and I loved it.

I didn't answer her. Instead, I pushed a finger inside her at an achingly slow pace. She writhed on my hand, but I used the other to hold her hips in place.

I pressed my lips against her clit again and finally answered her. "You've been a bad girl, Ms. Moore."

She whimpered and I flicked her clit with my tongue.

"Please, Jase."

God. That was the sexiest thing I had ever heard in my entire life.

I sucked her clit into my mouth one last time as I unbuttoned my pants. I needed to be inside her. I had to.

I lifted from my chair and she watched me as I lined myself up and slid inside her. She was arching off the desk, and her breasts were teasing me with the tiniest sliver of skin I could see above the edge of the fabric. For a moment, I considered ripping the whole damn thing off of her, but I remembered where we were and how quickly this could all go downhill.

I pressed my thumb against her clit and moved it in small circles as I pounded into her. She tightened around me, her pussy pulling out my pleasure, and I knew I wouldn't last much longer.

My office phone rang, and Sophie jumped underneath me. Annie's name lit up on the screen, and I knew I had to answer it before she barged into my office. Annie was the only other person who knew my code.

I pressed my hand against Sophie's mouth as I hit the intercom button. I thrust into her then answered Annie.

"Yeah?"

My voice sounded gruff even to my ears.

"Your one o'clock appointment is here."

I stared down into Sophie's eyes that looked wild with lust and the fear of being caught. I didn't stop thrusting into her, and she didn't stop lifting her hips to meet me.

"I'll be done in just a few moments." I barely managed to get the words out.

"You better be nice to that girl, Jase," Annie reprimanded

me, and I remembered that I was supposed to be going over Sophie's eval. "I like her."

"I am. Trust me."

"I don't trust you as far as I could throw you," Annie said before the phone clicked off.

"Oh my God." Sophie pressed her head back against the desk, and I slammed into her harder and faster while grinding my body against her clit.

It was only a moment later when she fell apart around me. I pressed my mouth against hers to swallow her cries, and I followed her over the edge as if her pleasure was somehow synced with mine.

We stayed like that, her arms wrapped around my back, my chest pressing against hers until she let out a small laugh. I leaned up and looked at her with a smile on my face. I had no idea what she was laughing at, but fuck, if it didn't sound good.

She pushed on my chest until I was fully standing then she pulled her dress down her legs.

"What's so funny?" I tucked myself into my pants and reached down to grab her panties.

"One." She held up her finger. "That's the second time we've fucked without a condom."

Shit. She was right. I hadn't even asked her if she was on birth control. I opened my mouth to do just that when she held up a second finger.

"Two. Annie gave you shit about being mean to me."

I handed her panties to her and buttoned my pants. "Annie gives me shit about everything." I tucked my shirt into my pants. "But are you?"

"Yes." She nodded her head. "I'm on birth control."

Thank God.

"Are you clean?" She stood from my desk and fixed her dress.

"Of course." I would never do something like that to her. "Are you?"

"No worries there, chief." She patted my chest.

She fluffed out her hair and I handed her the evaluation from my desk.

"This is the best evaluation that I've ever seen Tom give."

"Well, I'm happy to be of service." She winked at me then left my office as if she hadn't just rocked my world.

CHAPTER 13
SOPHIE

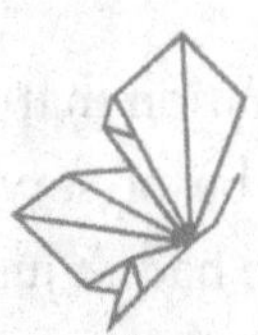

Jase found any opportunity he could to touch me.

Even if it was just a touch of his hand when we ran into each other in the break room or a quick caress of my ass when no one else was looking.

I didn't stop him as he pushed me against the door to my office and kissed me until I couldn't catch my breath.

And he sure as hell didn't stop me when I found him tucked away in his office with his brow scrunched in frustration and I dropped to my knees. I left his office with the taste of him on my tongue and thoughts of the way he cried out my name as he came in my mouth flooding my brain.

I hadn't been able to think about anything other than touching him.

It was Saturday afternoon, I was lying in bed watching Netflix like I had been doing all day, and all I could think about was getting back to work on Monday, so I could see him.

It was pathetic.

My phone dinged next to me, and I expected it to be

Kennedy who had been texting me all morning about the wedding. She and my brother would be in town on Friday then their wedding was only a week after that.

I couldn't wait to see them.

I searched through the blankets to find my phone and almost dropped it on my face when I saw Jase's name light up the screen.

Jase: Dinner?

Dinner. We didn't do dinner. Hell, we didn't do anything outside of the office.

Sophie: I didn't think we were the dinner kind of people.

There, that was simple and to the point.

Jase: As in the kind of people who eat?

I typed out a response then deleted it. Then I typed again.

Sophie: As in the kind of people who eat together.

I smiled down at my phone and watched those three little dots bounce over and over.

Jase: I can eat your pussy, but I'm not good enough to eat dinner with?

I almost choked on my spit as I read his words.

Sophie: I didn't say that.

God. I was saying that.

Jase: I'll make you a deal. Come eat dinner with me, and I promise that you won't be neglected because there's food.

I snorted and ran my finger over the keyboard. Did I want to have dinner with Jase? Yes. Did I think it was a bad idea? Also, yes.

Sophie: Where?

Jase: My house. 7 o'clock.

He didn't wait for another response. He messaged me his address, and I stared at it for a good five minutes before I pulled myself out of bed and jumped in the shower. I scrubbed and shaved every surface of my skin before I threw every item of clothing I owned onto my bed while trying to decide what to wear.

I showed up at his doorstep five minutes after seven. I could blame it on the fact that I didn't want to seem too eager, but the reality was that I tried on four different outfits and tried to talk myself out of coming at least three times.

Jase's house was nice. As in really nice. It was a two-story craftsman home that looked like Jase had probably decided on every detail from the ground up. The contrast of our lives was vividly apparent.

Jase answered the door wearing a pair of jeans and a smile.

I couldn't even look him in the face because I was far too busy trying to memorize every little detail of his chest and abs.

"Is that what you normally wear to dinner?" I still hadn't looked up at him, but his small laugh filled my ears.

"I just got out of the shower."

I looked up at him then and he wasn't lying. His short, dark hair was damp and looked like he had quickly run his hands through it. I had to stop myself from doing the same.

"Come in." He opened the door farther, and I stepped into his home.

It smelled like him. The whole house engulfed in that scent that I could never quite put my finger on.

He led me to the kitchen, and I took a seat at his large island while he checked something on the stove. I felt awkward. This felt awkward.

I didn't know how to be around him when we weren't fighting or tearing off each other's clothes.

"Tucker and Kennedy are going to be in town Tuesday." I had no idea why I said that. The last thing we needed in the already uncomfortable situation was mention of my brother.

"Yeah." He dipped his finger in the pan then brought it to his lips. "I talked to him earlier. They want us to go to dinner on Tuesday night."

"You told him about us?" My heart started racing.

"No." He turned to face me and leaned back against the counter. "He asked if we could meet them after we got off work."

"Oh." Of course, Tucker knew that we worked together. "That makes sense."

"Do you want me to tell him about us?" He said it so nonchalantly that it made me start to freak out for a second.

"What would you say? 'Oh hey, Tucker. By the way, your sister and I have been fucking in the office.'"

Jase grinned and took a step toward me, resting his elbows on the island. "And my kitchen island." He rubbed his hand over the granite. "And my bed." He leaned farther on the island and reached out to touch my fingers. "And hopefully the couch and the back deck."

My stomach tightened. "You're getting awfully hopeful there."

He shrugged his shoulders with a teasing smile. "A man can wish."

"And here I thought you were just inviting me over for dinner." I crossed my arms in fake indignation.

"You are here for dinner." He tapped his finger against my nose. "But you should always have dessert."

I laughed as he turned back to the stove. "Your house is gorgeous." I looked around the kitchen then to the large open space that led into the living room.

"Thank you." He drained a pot of pasta in the sink and steam billowed around him. "We just got finished building it a little over a year ago."

"So, that's a year's worth of ladies you've had here," I teased him. "If these new walls could talk."

He transferred the pasta into a large bowl. "They wouldn't have much to say." He smirked. "You're the first woman that's been here."

I snorted and crossed my arms. "You think I believe that I'm the first woman to come here."

"Come on." He motioned to the table with his bowl of pasta, and I followed him. "Technically, there have been other women here."

"Mmm hmm." I sat down in the seat he pulled out for me.

"But I wasn't interested in sleeping with any of them."

I looked up at him over my shoulder, and he surprised me when he presses a gentle kiss against my lips.

"Annie. Mrs. Norman. Oh." He snapped his fingers. "Your mom's been here."

"Do you have some sort of rule against bringing women to your house?"

Jase served me the delicious-looking pasta with some sort of cream sauce, and I moaned as I took the first bite.

"Not a rule per se. I just haven't liked anyone enough to bring them back to my house."

"Jase Hale." I put my hand over my heart. "You flatter me."

He rolled his eyes with laughter on his lips. "There goes your head."

"I can't help it if I'm the best you've ever had." I gave him a teasing smile and stuffed my mouth with another bite. "This is amazing." I pointed at my pasta with my fork. "Where did you learn to cook?"

"It was a necessity." He shrugged his shoulders. "My dad wasn't much of one."

Jase grew up with his father, and I honestly only remember meeting him a few times. Jase was always at our house. It wasn't the other way around.

"Well, it paid off." I ran my thumb over my chin to wipe away sauce. "I could eat my weight in this."

"What's your specialty?" He was watching me while he ate, and his green eyes somehow made me feel comfortable and intimidated at the same time.

"As in what?" I joked. "I'm pretty good at blow jobs." I cupped my hand around my mouth as if I was sharing a secret. "Or so I've heard."

He smirked at me. "I know you're good with your mouth. I meant with your hands."

I started to make an inappropriate gesture, but he interrupted me.

"In the kitchen." He chuckled.

"Oh." I waved my hand like that was nothing. "I can't cook anything."

He covered his mouth with his napkin and choked out a cough. "Nothing?"

"Not a damn thing." I popped more of his delicious pasta in my mouth. "Unless you count noodles in a cup."

He shook his head. "I most certainly do not."

"Then I'm guessing you don't count that macaroni and cheese where you add the water either."

"Your mom is an amazing cook." He acted like I was telling him that I was really an axe murderer.

"Your point? That didn't mean I learned to cook. It just meant that I ate well. This ass." I pointed my fork down in that direction. "You can thank her for that."

"I will." He bent to the side to get a look at said ass. "The next time I see her."

"Whatever." I rolled my eyes. "You wouldn't want to ruin my momma's perfect image of you."

"I can't help it your mom has good taste." He leaned back in his chair and my gaze trailed down his still exposed stomach.

"She does." I stabbed the last few pieces of pasta in my bowl. "She's just a bit misguided."

"How so?"

"She thinks you're sweet and charming, and I'm pretty sure she thinks you feed the poor."

That was an exaggeration but not much.

"And you?" He cocked an eyebrow.

"I'm just here for the food and the abs." I waved my fork in the direction of his perfect sculpted stomach. "Oh, and your penis."

He placed his hand over his heart. "Is that all I'm good for?"

"That has yet to be determined."

He stood from his chair and moved toward me. I squealed at the determination in his eyes as he wrapped his hands around my waist. He didn't waste any time as he lifted me out of my chair and pulled me toward him. My body was aligned with his, and the heat of his bare chest under my hands made my heart race.

"I guess I need to give you a reminder that I'm more than just my penis."

I trailed my fingers down his chest and smiled as his abs tightened under my touch. "I said abs too."

He gripped behind my knees and lifted me in the air. My arms wrapped around his shoulders so I wouldn't fall, and I laughed against his neck. "Where are you taking me?"

He didn't answer me. He tugged my body closer to his and started walking. I had no idea where we were going, but I didn't care.

The cool air of the night hit my bare arms as he carried me to the back porch, and I quickly looked around. It was dark, but I could still make out what was around me by the glow of the kitchen lights inside.

I was expecting him to throw me down on the ground and make me tell him how amazing he was, but he apparently had other plans.

He set me down in a white rocking chair and pushed some hair out of my face.

"Are you kicking me out because of the penis comment? I said it was impressive."

"No." He shook his head then kissed my forehead. "I'm going to make you a fire."

He waved toward the fire pit that sat in front of the chairs, and I fanned my face.

"Fire? I don't know how I'll handle it. I've never seen a man make fire before."

He smiled and squatted down next to the pit. "Then prepare to be amazed."

He stuck his hand somewhere under the fire pit and turned a little nob. Instantly the fire came to life.

I couldn't stop laughing.

"I'm happy to know we'd survive in the wilderness if we ever got lost."

"Are you planning on getting lost out in the woods with me?" He pulled his chair right next to mine and sat down.

"No, but you never know. Zombie apocalypse and all that. What are you going to do? Carry around your little fake fire."

"If I need to." He turned his head to the side to look at me. "But you do know that they make lighters now, I wouldn't have to rub two rocks together."

"Thank God." I laughed and looked around. The view from his back porch had to be amazing during the day because I could still make out the shape of the mountains in the dark. I would spend all my time out here if I was him. "Is that a boat?"

He followed my gaze to the big-ass boat that was parked near his garage. "It is."

"Who knew." I rocked back in my chair. "You may be pretty useful after all."

He rolled his eyes. "Do you want me to take you out on my boat?"

"Of course, I do. What kind of woman do you think I am?"

"One who is too far away." He grinned and tugged my hand toward him.

"The only way I'm getting closer to you is if I'm in your lap." The arm of his rocking chair was practically rubbing against mine.

"That's our only option? Damn." He smirked and tugged on my hand again until I had no choice but to stand.

He was looking up at me, and I swear if I hadn't already steeled my heart against him, it would be so easy to fall.

He tugged on my hand gently, and I placed one knee beside his thigh before lifting the other and settling myself in his lap. This was where I was most comfortable with him. Being physical with Jase was easy. It was everything else that seemed to fuck me up.

I ground my hips down against his, and he stared up at me. He wrapped his hand in my hair and brought my face down to meet his. His lips were gentle as they met mine, too gentle, so I leaned back and pulled my shirt over my head.

His gaze flicked to my chest as if he couldn't stop himself, and I took advantage of his momentary distraction to kiss him like I needed him to kiss me.

There was no gentleness in this kiss. He matched my pace, and his fingers dug into my sides as he pulled me closer to him even as our skin already touched.

He made quick work of removing my bra, and chill bumps broke out across my skin as the night air hit my nipples. Jase wrapped his arms around my back pulling me closer, and I arched into him as his fingers ran up and down my spine.

I was beyond turned on, and even though both of our jeans were still in place, this somehow felt more erotic than any other time before.

I rolled my hips against him, and he pulled his mouth away from mine and pressed it against my neck. He took his time. I felt him everywhere.

His mouth moved lazily down my neck. His tongue traced a path that made me feel like I was coming out of my skin.

By the time he finally made it to my breasts, I would have done anything to make him give me more.

He stood from his chair with me wrapped around him.

"Where are we going now?" I was breathless, and he was the one doing all the work.

"I want you in my bed." His words were forced out against my skin.

"It's too far away." I squirmed and tried to roll my hips against him.

He didn't listen to me though. He continued to kiss my neck as he carried me back into the house.

He wasn't watching where he was going. His tongue flicked out against my nipple, and I threw my head back just as he sucked it into his mouth. He kicked something that made a loud crash, and I laughed, a breathless needy laugh, as my back slammed into the wall.

Jase dropped me to my feet, only long enough to pull my pants from my body, then he lifted my thighs back around his waist.

I couldn't catch my breath as he leaned into me and kissed me like he was dying to remember the taste of my lips and the soft sounds of my moans. I had never been kissed like that in my life. Not with such unrestrained hunger.

There was no question whether Jase wanted me or not.

He left no room for confusion.

His hand pushed off the wall, his lips still on mine, and he started moving through the house again. I knew we finally made it to his room when my back hit his mattress, and I sat up on my elbows to watch him pop the button of his jeans before he slowly pulled them and his boxers down his legs.

It was the first time I had ever seen Jase fully naked.

I had fucked him and blown him and come on his tongue, but this was different.

There was nothing between us. No clothes, no office, and no rushing to not be caught.

It made my stomach tighten and the urge to run was overwhelming.

He didn't give me time to let that fear take over. He kneeled on the bed between my thighs, and he pressed a kiss just on the inside of my knee. I took a deep breath and told myself that this was the same Jase. This was the same kind of sex, and I would leave after, just the same as I did in his office.

He crawled up the mattress, and I looked up at him and the way his body covered mine. He was always handsome, but like this, here with me, he was something more.

I lifted my hand and let my fingers run down the skin of his stomach. His body shuddered under my touch, but Jase kept his eyes on me. I let my hand fall, and he leaned down and pressed a kiss just at the base of my sternum.

"Jase." I whispered his name. I didn't know what I was asking, but he did.

He leaned forward and pressed his mouth to mine. He

gripped his cock in his hand and rubbed it through my slit. I would have been embarrassed by how wet I was if I didn't swallow his deep groan of appreciation in my mouth.

He didn't waste any time.

I bit down on his bottom lip as he slid into me, and there was something about feeling him above me without anything between us that made it feel so much better than it ever had before.

He leaned up and gripped my thigh in one of his hands. He brought it forward, opening me up to him, and he watched our connection as he moved in and out of me.

My body ached from the pressure that was building inside of me, and I tried to look anywhere but at him. He was moving inside me at a pace that would normally bore me, but every time he pushed inside me, my legs started shaking harder and harder.

I couldn't fall apart underneath him like this.

It was too much. Too vulnerable.

I pushed on his chest and flipped him over on his back. I moved on top of him before he could utter a word, but he let out a low growl as I settled down against him taking him deeper than I ever had before.

I started to move against him, and he let me. He was staring up at me as I rolled my hips against him, so I pressed my fingers into his abs and threw my head back as he hit a spot inside of me that would have me coming faster than a virgin boy on prom night.

My gaze jumped back to his as he sat up and wrapped his arms around me. He was refusing to give me the space I needed. He was refusing to let me hide.

I would have moved again if I wasn't so close to coming. I would have changed positions to where he had no choice but to look at the back of my head, but Jase was lifting me off of him with the strength of his arms and slamming me back down on him with a force that was driving me wild.

I gripped his face in my hands and he looked up at me for a split second before I pressed my lips against his almost painfully. He matched my kiss. Two people falling apart around each other grasping for that last moment of control.

There was no space between us. My chest was against his chest. My stomach trembled against his.

Jase slammed me down against him harder and faster, and I lifted on my knees to help him. I was falling, hard and fast, and I couldn't stop it if I wanted to.

But I didn't want to.

All I could think about was him. Nothing else mattered in that moment. Not work. Not my damn brother. Nothing.

I fell apart around him, and he held me against him tightly as he lost his own control beneath me.

I didn't move as he lay back down and held me to his chest. I just breathed him in as I ran my finger along the crease of his elbow. Neither one of us said a word. We were both trying to catch our breath, and I was trying to calm my racing heart.

He pushed my hair out of my face and combed his fingers through it before they gently fell to my back. I tried to follow the path of his fingers, tried to decipher the small patterns he traced across my skin, but I was too comfortable, and my eyes were too heavy.

The last thing I remember is Jase pressing a small kiss to the top of my head right before I fell asleep.

CHAPTER 14
JASE

Sophie was sleeping like the dead.

I woke up with her body still wrapped around mine, and for the first time in my entire life, I didn't panic.

I had only fallen asleep after sex on two different occasions and both of them involved alcohol.

But this was different. Sophie passed out on my chest so quickly that I couldn't ask her to leave if I wanted to. I didn't want to.

I didn't even want to move an inch because I was scared she'd wake up and freak. Her eyes were clouded with her worry all night. We were used to sneaked kisses and quick fucks. Last night was nothing like that.

I didn't plan for it to happen that way either.

All I knew was that I hadn't stopped thinking about her since I left work on Friday, and I was jonesing to get back into the office and it had nothing to do with work. It was pathetic.

I was pussy-whipped. Plain and simple.

Breaking my own rules was something I never did, but Sophie was making me destroy every damn one of them.

I didn't sleep with women I worked with.

I sure as hell didn't bring them back to my house.

I didn't sleep with them more than two nights in a row.

And I never fucked without a condom.

Simple. Easy. And one hundred percent fucked when it came to her.

But I didn't feel like I was breaking the rules. It was fun and harmless, and both of us knew where we stood.

Sure, the sex got a bit intense last night, but that didn't change anything.

Sophie had made it perfectly fucking clear that I was nothing more than sex to her. If that was all I could get, then that was what I would take. Wanting more wasn't my thing. It didn't matter that I thought about her all the time or that I had more fun with her than I had in a very long time.

This was Sophie we were talking about.

She had hated me for so long. Hell, I had hated her, but it was different now.

Hating Sophie? That shit was easy. She made it so.

Whatever was happening right now. It was harder.

I didn't know where the line was drawn. No one at work could know about us, that was a given, but would she go back to acting like she hated me when her brother got in town?

I tried to not let myself think about that. We had less than one week before he got here, and I planned to enjoy every spare second of Sophie that I could.

When she walked out into the kitchen wearing one of my t-shirts, I almost dropped the spatula in my hand.

My God, she was gorgeous.

Her hair was piled on the top of her head and her eyes were still a bit dreamy from sleep, and I momentarily wondered what it would be like to wake up to her like this on a regular basis.

"Good morning." I pulled the bacon out of the pan and put it on our plates with the eggs.

"Morning." One arm was crossed over her chest, and she ran her hand up and down the opposite arm. "Coffee?"

I pointed to the pot on the counter, and she quickly made her way over and poured a cup. I walked up behind her and leaned forward to set the creamer next to the sugar.

Her back straightened the tiniest bit, and I took a second to take in the long curve of her back beneath my shirt while she fixed her coffee. She turned so she was facing me and brought the cup to her lips.

We watched each other for a second before we started to talk at the same time.

"Breakfast is ready."

"I'm sorry I fell asleep."

We stopped at the same time, and she smiled at me before tugging on the edge of my shirt that hit her mid-thigh. "I couldn't find my shirt."

I reached forward and toyed with the same edge she was tugging. "I'm pretty sure it's still on the porch."

"Ah." She took another sip of her coffee. "I forgot about that."

"I didn't." I arched a brow at her.

She rolled her eyes. "You know what I mean."

"I cooked breakfast." I nodded over my shoulder, but I could already see her withdrawing.

"I should probably head home." She set her coffee cup down on the counter, and I knew that if I didn't say anything, she would be out the door as soon as she found her clothes.

"You want to go to a baseball game?"

"What?"

I don't know why I asked her that. Of course, she didn't want to go to some damn baseball game. "I got the tickets from a client. It's a semi-pro league, but there's free beer and food."

She bit her lip, and I knew she was considering it.

"Free beer and a bunch of men in baseball pants?" She cocked an eyebrow.

"Yeah." I grinned at her. "Not to mention the best date around." I pointed to my chest.

She looked me over from head to toe. "Uh huh."

"You don't think so?" I took a step toward her and she stepped back until her back pressed against the counter.

"Like the best ever?" She turned her head as if she was considering. "If I had to pick between you and a Hemsworth brother..."

"You'd pick a Hemsworth over me?" I put my hand against my bare chest.

"Hello." She rolled her eyes. "Have you seen *Thor*? Do you know how easily he could throw me around and have his way with me?"

Of course that's why she would pick Thor. "Do you need a reminder?"

She tapped her chin. "A reminder of what?"

I moved toward her and gripped her hips in my hands before I lifted her onto the counter. Her legs fell open on their own accord, and I settled between them. I kissed her jaw before moving my mouth to her ear.

I nipped her earlobe, causing her to moan quietly before I said, "I can have my own way with you."

I watched the corner of her mouth lift into a smile. "Prove it."

So, I did. I jerked her legs forward until her ass barely rested on the counter and leaned her back. Then I made her forget everything except screaming my name.

CHAPTER 15
SOPHIE

I probably shouldn't have said yes.

Going to his house when I knew that sex was going to be involved? That didn't seem to tiptoe across the line as much as spending a Sunday afternoon with him did. But I didn't have any other plans, and if I was being honest, I really wanted to go.

Jase had taken his time with me on the kitchen counter. By the time he was done, my throat was raw from screaming his name and my legs felt like they might collapse as I walked to the table to eat the breakfast he made me.

Once I got home to get ready for the baseball game, I was full, sated, and too happy to not freak out just a bit.

He was Jase Hale for crying out loud.

He wasn't going to be my happily ever after, but man, I was happy right now. As long as I remembered that this was temporary, this infatuation with each other, everything would be fine.

Jase picked me up outside of my parents' house, and I ran out and jumped in his car before either one of them could ask questions. That was exactly what I didn't need. Nosey parents bursting my bubble.

Jase's eyes went straight to my legs as I closed the car door behind me, and instantly I knew that my cutoff jean shorts were the right way to go. I was hoping he wouldn't be too dressed up considering I was wearing ratty shorts, a pair of Chucks, and a plain white t-shirt, but Jase dressed down was even worse.

He had on a pair of jeans with an old Smokey's Baseball t-shirt that had a tiny little hole at the seam of his shoulder, and a baseball cap sat on his head backward.

Jase in his work clothes was hot.

This Jase, this was my every teenage fantasy come to life.

"You ready?" He smiled over at me as he shifted the gear in to reverse.

"Yes." I couldn't help but feel giddy. I knew it was dangerous, but in that moment, I didn't care.

The baseball stadium was buzzing with people, vendors, and excitement when we arrived. Jase grabbed my hand as he pulled me through the crowd, and I let him. His fingers tightened around mine as he guided me toward the gift shop, and I laughed as he pointed to the foam finger that was displayed in the corner.

I made the mistake of telling him that I had never been to a big baseball game like this on the way over here. Football? Sure. But baseball wasn't a huge thing at my school.

"Do you know anything about baseball?" he asked.

Apparently telling him I knew that there were loads of foam fingers in the crowd was the wrong thing to say.

Of course, I knew more about baseball than that. I had been forced to watch the sport with my dad and Tucker plenty of times, but I wasn't lying about the foam fingers either.

"Are you really buying a foam finger?" I laughed as Jase let go of my hand to pull his wallet out of his pocket.

"How can I give you an authentic first baseball experience if I don't?" I pointed out something else to the cashier. "We'll need one of those shirts too."

I didn't realize he meant for me until he held it up against my chest. "Perfect."

It looked like it was a good size too big, but I didn't argue. Instead, I went to the bathroom to change shirts and had to tie the end in a small knot at my stomach because it was so long. Jase tracked my every movement as I walked out and pushed my way through all the people to get to him. He licked his lips, almost unnoticeably, as he looked over the baseball shirt he had just bought me then he pointed at me with that damn foam finger that covered his hand.

"How did a baseball shirt somehow make you hotter?"

I put my hands on my hips as I moved closer to him. There were so many people walking by us, but I didn't know any of them. It was almost like we were in our own secret bubble. It didn't matter what we did here. There was no one to catch us. No one here to judge us.

"You think I'm hot?" I pressed my body against his and ran my finger over that small hole in his shirt.

"Of course I do." He wrapped his arms around me, and the tip of the foam finger hit the back of my bare thighs. He leaned in close so his mouth was right next to my ear. "I'd rip that fucking thing off you if there weren't so many people around."

"Why be shy now?" I batted my eyes at him jokingly, but he looked dead serious.

"Because I'd have to kick every one of these motherfuckers' asses when they looked at you. I'm already tempted to now."

My heart launched into my throat and I looked around us. The only person looking at me was him.

"You're insane." I ran my finger over the stubble on his jaw. It was the first time since I started working at Norman Architecture that I had seen him with it. "Nobody is looking at me."

He leaned down just slightly and pressed his lips to mine in a fleeting kiss. "Trust me. They all are."

I knew that he was flattering me, but it didn't matter. My stomach still tightened and my heart began to race.

"Let's go find our seats." He nodded toward the doorway that led out to the field.

"Okay." I nodded my head and followed him.

I took my seat beside him. We were sitting just behind the dugout on one side of the field, and the team was already lining up for the national anthem. Jase tried to tell me what was going on, and I thought it was cute that he thought I was truly that clueless. He was so into it though. He told me how many strikes and balls the batter got, and he pointed to each base telling me which one was first, second, and third.

I almost died laughing, but he was so relaxed with a beer in his hand and his feet up on the railing.

The game was already started, and I loved the excitement that was in the air. The batter hit the ball to our shortstop who fumbled the ball before tossing it to the second baseman for an out.

The crowd around us was on their feet and there were grumbles of frustration even though the game just started a few minutes before.

I decided to join them. "Come on, shortstop," I yelled toward the field. "That should have been a double play."

Jase looked at the field and back at me. "You?" He looked back to the field. "You know about baseball?"

"I do have a brother." I grinned and took a sip of my beer.

"I just explained the bases to you."

"It was very interesting too." I clapped with the crowd as the next batter got struck out. "But I learned about the different bases years ago." I winked at him.

He chuckled around the rim of his beer. "Well damn."

I waved my hand in his direction. "I never have had a foam finger though."

"So, you're saying that at least I'm your first foam finger?"

"Exactly." I knocked a bit of my beer over the edge of my cup with said foam finger. "You were almost my first everything."

He looked over at me like I was crazy. "You told me you weren't a virgin."

I leaned my head to the side. "I don't think I said that specifically."

"You insinuated it." He narrowed his eyes at me.

I waved off his concern with my giant foam finger. "It doesn't matter. It was a long time ago."

"Who did you lose your virginity to?" His playful attitude was gone, and he was staring at me like he needed to know the answer.

I didn't want to answer, so I threw his questions right back at him. "Who did you lose your virginity to?"

He didn't hesitate. "Jessica Bledsoe. Tenth grade."

I tensed. I didn't expect him to actually tell me, and I

also didn't expect that I wouldn't like the answer. Jessica Bledsoe was a total bitch in high school.

"Thank you for telling me." I turned back to the game.

"Oh no." He gripped my hand and leaned forward to catch my gaze. "I told you, now you tell me."

"I don't remember agreeing to that." I shook my head.

"Soph." He practically growled my name.

"Elliott Dalton." I winced as I said his name. It was by far the worst sexual experience of my life, and I don't think it had anything to do with the fact that I was a virgin. Me being a virgin plus intoxicated plus heartbroken over Jase? That equaled a winning combination when combined with an overly eager teenage boy who had no idea what he was doing.

"That guy from your birthday?"

"That would be the one." I laughed.

"Fuck, Sophie." He ran his hand down his face.

I waved off his concern. "It doesn't matter."

"It does."

Right at that moment, one of our players hit the ball over the fence and the crowd went wild. I joined them, jumping to my feet to celebrate and avoid Jase. He knew it too, but he let me.

I didn't want to go back and think about the night I lost my virginity or how I regretted it for far too long.

I held up my foam finger to high-five Jase, and a little of his irritation slipped as he smacked his hand against mine.

He didn't bring it up again after that. He got us both some hot dogs and a couple more beers from the vendor who was walking up and down the aisles. I had to take off my foam finger long enough to eat, and Jase laughed when I pouted about it.

We settled back into our usual banter, the easy push and pull without digging any further. I breathed easier as he smiled at me, and I crossed my legs underneath me as I cheered along with the crowd.

It was just after the fourth inning when the crowd got louder than they had before. I looked around me to see what was going on, and Jase pointed to the jumbotron. There, centered in a large red heart, was an older man and woman. The crowd cheered for them to kiss, and the lady blushed before her husband pulled her closer to him and laid one on her.

I cheered and catcalled with the crowd as the camera moved to another couple. This one was much younger, and the girl didn't hesitate as she grabbed her man's face and kissed him. I'm pretty sure there was even a bit of tongue.

The next one showed what looked like a dad and his daughter. She laughed when she saw herself on screen, and her dad peppered kisses along her face causing her to giggle.

I laughed along with her until I saw my own face light up on the screen. I ducked my head a bit, but the people sitting around us went crazy. I looked over at Jase who was staring at me with a stupid happy smile on his face, and he didn't think twice before he wrapped his hands in my hair and pressed his lips against mine. The arm of my seat was digging into my side as he pulled me closer to him, but I didn't care.

He kissed me like he meant it. There was no reserve due to the fact that we were currently plastered across a huge screen for everyone to see. When he finally pulled away from me, the people around us were clapping, whistling, and cheering like we were their favorite couple in the world.

But we weren't a couple.

Little did they know that we were practically two strangers who really liked to fuck each other.

I knew that was unfair. We were more than that.

We had always been more than that.

But this still felt like madness.

He was my boss, he was my brother's best friend, but I had never craved a touch so much until I felt his.

It was insane, but sanity felt overrated.

We ended up losing the game six to seven, but I was still smiling as we left the stadium. The crowd was grumbling about what this player or that player should have done, but my hand was clasped in Jase's and we pushed through the mass of people until we finally made it to the sidewalk.

"That was awesome." I leaned against his arm as we made our way to the car.

"You do realize that we lost, right?" He didn't care that we lost. He was smiling just as much as I was.

"That's what those numbers meant?" I twirled my hair between my fingers.

"Okay, smart-ass." He lifted me in his arms and twirled me around while I laughed. "I can't believe you let me believe you didn't know anything about baseball."

He set me back on my feet, but I didn't feel like it.

"You were so cute with your mansplaining." I bopped his nose with my finger.

"I was not mansplaining." He rolled his eyes. "I thought you really needed help."

"You all usually do."

He reached out to grab me, but this time I moved out of his reach.

"Now, now, Mr. Hale." I wagged my finger at him. "Is that any way to treat one of your employees?"

His eyes clouded over for just a second and I instantly regretted reminding him of who we were. He quickly shook it off.

"Not all of my employees." He smirked at me. "But you're special."

"Oh yeah?" I walked backward so I could still look at him. "Like employee of the month?"

He chuckled and reached out for me before I tripped over the uneven concrete. "Something like that."

"This will break Annie's heart. She told me she's been your employee of the month since she started."

He shrugged his shoulders. "Annie takes care of me, but you." He toyed with my fingers in his hand. "You really take care of me."

I smacked at his chest. "You make me sound like some sort of prostitute."

"You know." He tapped his chin. "Secretly, *Pretty Woman* is one of my favorite movies."

"You aren't loaded enough for this to be a *Pretty Woman* situation."

"Damn." He unlocked his car and walked me to my door. He didn't open it right away, instead he leaned forward and pressed my back against the warm exterior. He was staring down at my lips, and I wrapped my hand in his t-shirt to pull him closer to me. "Does that mean I don't get to climb up your fire escape?"

He was holding himself just an inch away from my mouth, and I was desperate for him to close the space. "My dad might catch you."

"Your dad loves me." He ran his thumb along my bottom lip. "He'd probably pack you up himself."

"It's good to know that no matter how much you've changed, that ego is still in check."

He grinned and moved his lips closer to mine. I could feel the movement of them against me. "You've always loved my ego."

"Don't get ahead of yourself." I started to lean back to look up at him, but he leaned forward and silenced me with his lips.

I wrapped my arms around his neck, and he pressed his body fully against mine. It wasn't enough. I wanted more of him. I needed more.

He didn't move his arms off the car where they rested beside my head no matter how hard I pulled him closer to me. There was fire in his kiss, and I was melting around him.

When he pulled away, I felt off-balance, and I didn't let myself consider why I felt more like myself in that moment than I ever had before.

CHAPTER 16
JASE

Dragging my ass into work the next morning was torture. If I hadn't known that she would be here, I may have even played hooky.

I never played hooky. Ever.

But Sophie made me feel reckless.

Nothing about us was right, but that lack of reason did nothing to deter me.

It only seemed to fuel my craving for her.

When I had dropped her back off at her house last night, the smile on her face was genuine and the lightness of her mood was contagious. Neither one of us wanted to say good-bye. This weekend had just been me and her. We didn't have to worry about our coworkers or siblings or false pretenses. It was just us, and it made me want more.

I fucking needed it.

I tried to shake off the thoughts of Sophie that were clouding every inch of my head and focus on my work.

Our teams were going to be presenting their plans for the Anderson Development this week, and the first team of overachievers announced that they were ready to present today. Mr. Norman was excited to see the first set of plans, and I should have been too. This project would be huge for us if we managed to land it.

We had to land it.

I walked into the conference room and took a seat next to Mr. Norman. The team in front of us, Ken's team, was sorting out their plans and setting up their presentation.

"How's Sophie?" Mr. Norman asked before taking a sip of his coffee.

"Why?" I asked the question before I could think better of it. "I mean Tom says she's doing okay."

"Uh huh." He arched one of his eyebrows that was peppered in grey at me.

"What does that mean?" I turned my chair toward him so no one else could hear us.

"It doesn't mean anything. I was just asking." He was smirking.

"Bullshit." I tapped my pen against my desk. "Say what you mean, old man."

He rubbed his chin and leaned back in the chair. "Erin and I like her."

"You all made that perfectly clear the other day. I thought you were going to offer her my job." I rolled my eyes. I was fucking with him. I loved that they liked Sophie. It mattered to me a little bit too much actually.

"No way." He put his hand on my shoulder and squeezed. "She needs at least a year under her belt first."

I rolled my eyes and Ken cleared his throat to start their presentation.

It was good. If not a bit expected, and my thoughts kept

jumping back to Sophie's own plans she had been doodling. They were better than this, by far.

Mr. Norman thanked them for their presentation and told them we'll have an answer toward the end of the week. He's so much better at this than I am. I was about ready to tell them to go back to the drawing table.

Every other company in this entire business would have those exact plans. We needed to stand out. We needed to be bold.

"That kind of sucked," I said to him when the door finally closed behind Ken's team.

"A bit." He smiled and stood. "Let's go see Sophie."

He was already headed toward the door while I tried to gather the presentation packets left in front of us. I finally caught up to him when he was right at the edge of Sophie's office door.

"Anyone home?" His loud voice bellowed down the hall as he knocked on her door.

"Dan!" Her voice was cheerful, and she sounded just as excited to see him. "What are you doing here?"

I rounded the door to her office just as he pulled her into a hug. "Jase made me come in. Apparently, I haven't been working enough."

Her smiling eyes found mine. "He's a slave driver, that one."

I huffed and sat on the arm of one of her chairs.

She turned her attention back to him. "How is Erin?"

"She's good." He nodded his head. "She keeps asking when you're going to have a girls' day with her."

"Let me get through my brother's wedding then I'm all hers."

I arched an eyebrow at her teasingly, but she avoided

looking at me. The edge of her lips popped up just slightly at the corner, and I knew she saw it.

"She'll be happy to hear it." Mr. Norman turned toward me. "She used to talk about Jase all the damn time, but it seems he's been replaced."

I put my hand over my heart as Sophie laughed. "You tell her that I'm gutted. I thought I was her favorite."

Sophie's gaze dragged over me slowly. "We can't all be the favorite, Jase." She shrugged her shoulder. "You've had a good run."

Mr. Norman chuckled and put his arm around her shoulders. "He has, hasn't he. He needs someone giving him a run for his money."

"Oh, she most certainly does that."

Sophie blushed at my words, but Mr. Norman chuckled.

"Alright, I have to get out of here. Erin will kill me if I'm here too long." He patted his right hip. "Apparently this hip needs a bit of rest to heal."

"Well, you better listen to her." Sophie looked up at him. "Erin knows what she's talking about."

"Oh Lord." Mr. Norman walked toward the door. "I don't need you ganging up on me too."

"I told you." I leaned back on the chair so I could still see him as he walked out. "More trouble than they're worth."

Mr. Norman's laugh echoed into Sophie's office.

"Is that so?" Sophie put her hands on her hips.

I smirked at her and shrugged my shoulders. "Tell me you aren't trouble."

"I'm not trouble." Her hip cocked to the side just slightly, and I smiled. Trouble never looked so goddamn fine.

"What are you then?" I crossed my ankles and let my eyes roam over her.

"I'm fun." She took a step toward me but stopped as her eyes went to her open office door.

"Fun?" I cocked an eyebrow and stood.

"You don't think I'm fun?" She watched me as I took a step closer to her.

"Oh, you're fun." My voice was quiet enough for only her to hear. "And gorgeous."

"Jase." She said my name as if that would somehow make me stop my advance and her eyes darted to the door.

"And smart." I ran my finger over hers for just a second, and her body tensed. "And so damn sassy."

She shoved my shoulder and tried to hide her small smile.

"Get out of my office."

"I don't want to." I walked behind her until I was just behind her and had a clear view of the door. If someone looked in here, we looked innocent enough. She wasn't touching me, but fuck, I was dying to touch her. "I want to kiss every inch of you." My fingers grazed the small of her back with a barely there touch and her breath caught. "Do you think you'll taste the same as you did yesterday? Will I be able to still taste me across your skin?"

She looked over her shoulder just slightly, but her harsh breath mingled with mine. "Try it and see." She licked her bottom lip, and if I could taste the wickedness on her tongue in that moment, I knew I wouldn't be able to stop.

"You're fucking trouble, Ms. Moore." I ran my thumb along her bottom lip then forced myself to leave her office.

CHAPTER 17
SOPHIE

My brother was back in town.

I knew I should have been excited. He was my brother after all, and he was about to marry one of the coolest girls I had ever met. But I couldn't stop thinking about Jase, or more importantly, how things would change between us with Tucker in town.

I wasn't a fucking kid anymore. If Tucker had a problem with me and Jase, he could get over it. It wasn't like he needed to protect my virtue or his friend.

We were two consenting adults.

But I knew Jase cared.

And that bothered me.

But right now, all I could think about was getting out of this office. I had sneaked into Jase's office for a bit of "advice" this morning, and I swear I could still feel his touch on my body as if he had burned me. We were being careless around the office, too careless, but I couldn't seem to stop myself.

When I saw him, the desire to touch him was too much. It was foreplay all on its own, being so close to him, being surrounded by his smell, being so fucking close to his touch, but not being able to do anything about it.

It was a sweet torture and one hell of a game.

When he winked at me when he thought no one was looking, my thighs tightened. When he touched me so no one else could see, I could barely breathe.

Tom was droning on and on about the presentation tomorrow. It would be my last day before I was off for my brother's wedding, and I let the excitement of everything around me get to my head.

"I've been drawing up my own presentation."

Tom's eyes slid to me with pure ice.

I held up my hands. "Just to practice." I handed him the plans that I had tucked neatly against my lap and tried to breathe. I hadn't planned to show him. Hell, I hadn't planned to show anyone, but I figured I'd never get anywhere if he didn't think I had potential.

I was interested in his critique. Nothing more.

Tom looked over my plans with an expression that still bordered on angry before he set them to the side. "I don't have time for your practice right now."

"Sure." I nodded my head. Of course, he didn't have time.

He continued on as if I hadn't even spoken and the team decided to go with his plans for the presentation. I personally thought Sean's plans were better, but there was no way in hell I was voicing that opinion.

Especially not now.

My phone vibrated in my lap, and I quickly checked it as Tom talked.

Jase: Are you ready for dinner?

I looked up to make sure Tom wasn't paying attention to me, which was a waste of my time and messaged him back.

Sophie: If Tom will ever stop talking, yes.

Jase: Tell him his boss said to can it.
You've got somewhere to be.

I wiped my hand against my skirt as it started to sweat.

Sophie: I'll get right on that. I'm sure that would go over really well.

Those three little dots danced across my screen instantly as if he was waiting for my reply.

Jase: I'll see you there?

I read his words over and over again in my head. Of course, he would see me there. But did he mean that he'd see me there as friends. Me, Tucker's sister, and him, Tucker's best friend.

I didn't know how to act. I didn't know what to say.

Sophie: Yeah.

He didn't text me back after that, and my thumb bounced over the screen as I considered texting him.

"I'll see you all in the morning." I clicked off my phone as Tom spoke. "Make sure you are all on time." He looked around at each one of us as if we were normally late.

I grabbed my stuff and headed out of that office before he could find something else that had to be done before the morning.

When I finally walked into the restaurant, everyone else was already there.

Kennedy jumped out of her chair as soon as she saw me, and we pulled each other in a tight hug. I hadn't seen her or my brother in months, and it felt even longer than that.

"Finally," my brother joked before he pushed his own chair back and held me against his chest. "Jase been riding you too hard these days?"

My face instantly flamed, and my eyes found Jase's. He was sitting directly across from my brother, and there next to him was the open seat for me. "He's definitely not giving me any special treatment."

He rolled his eyes and the corner of his mouth lifted in a smirk.

"Jase Hale," Kennedy scolded him. "You better be nice to Sophie. I'll kick your ass."

"Kennedy, babe." Jase turned his attention on her, and I had no idea how she seemed so unfazed under the weight of his smile.

"Don't you 'Kennedy, babe' me." She pointed her finger at him. "I don't fall for your charms like all these trollops of yours."

I avoided looking at either or them and pulled out of my brother's embrace.

"Missed you." He tugged on the end of my hair.

"Missed you too." I moved around the table and pulled the chair as far away from Jase as I could without being too noticeable.

"I don't have trollops." Jase took a sip of his drink. From the looks of it, tonight was a whiskey night.

"Okay, Jase." Kennedy rolled her eyes and adjusted her glasses. "And I'm really not that into reading."

"The fact that you have to compare Jase's whoring skills to your nerding skills makes me love you a little bit more." My brother pressed his lips to Kennedy's forehead, and I told myself not to think about Jase or his said whoring skills.

"Oh God." Jase pretended to raise his hand for the waiter. "I need another drink."

"For real, Soph." My brother turned his attention to me. "Has Jase been treating you okay?"

Jase bumped his knee against mine under the table, and I cleared my throat.

"He hasn't been a complete ass."

Jase chuckled, and my brother lifted his glass. "Looky there. Improvement. I honestly thought the two of you would have killed each other by now."

"Nah." Jase shook his head. "I couldn't kill her at work. I'd lose my job."

I rolled my eyes. "Plus, our boss likes me more than him."

"That's true." Jase chuckled and finished his drink.

"Any hot guys there?" Kennedy wagged her eyebrows at me.

"Just him." I nodded my head in Jase's direction. "He may be an ass, but he's got one as well."

Kennedy laughed, and Jase smirked at me.

"That's gross," my brother said just as Kennedy said, "He really does have a nice ass."

My brother turned to her, but she waved him off. "I'm almost married. I can talk about your best friend's ass."

"I don't think that's how that works." He chuckled.

"It should." I picked up a roll and tore off a piece. "Speaking of ass. You ready for your bachelorette party?"

Tucker looked between me and his fiancée. "What do you mean speaking of ass?"

"I'm not giving away the details." I popped a piece of bread in my mouth. Her bachelorette party has exactly zero things to do with ass unless Brooke, Kennedy's best friend, was planning a surprise, but I liked to keep my brother on his toes.

"Don't worry about it." Jase looked over at my brother. "Once we get to your bachelor party, you're not going to worry about them."

"I'll always worry about her." My brother looked at Kennedy again.

"Okay. Seriously." I held my hand in the air. "Waiter."

The waiter came to our table when he saw my hand, and I made him laugh when I told him I needed him to go ahead and bring me two margaritas to deal with my brother's love fest. He asked me if we wanted to have any food with our alcohol, and my brother told him yes before I could tell him to just keep the bread coming. We ordered our food, and I practically cheered when he came back with my drinks.

"What time does Brooke get in tomorrow?" I took a big long sip of my margarita.

"Noon. She and Liam are flying in together."

"Oh yeah." I fanned myself. Liam was another one of my brother's best friends, hot as hell, and cluelessly hot for Brooke. "I bet that will be an interesting flight."

"That's not happening." Tucker shook his head.

"*Okay.*" He was an idiot.

"You don't think I know who my best friends are fucking?"

Jase's hand touched the edge of my skirt. I jumped, just slightly.

"Kennedy, is it happening?" I barely managed to get out the words against the feel of his skin against mine.

"It's so happening." She smiled. "I bet they don't make it through the entire reception."

"You think they're going to fuck at our wedding?" Tucker looked at her like she was crazy.

"Everyone fucks at weddings, and those two have so much pent-up sexual tension. It's bound to happen. Brooke is hot. Right, Jase?" Kennedy looked to Jase for support.

As soon as the words left her lips, a tiny bit of jealousy ached in my chest. He hadn't even answered her damn question yet, but it was there just the same.

"Right," Jase answered casually with his cocky smile firmly in place.

I looked down at my drink, and his hand found my leg again. I didn't turn to look at him when his fingers pressed into my skin. Instead, I smiled at my brother and Kennedy.

"If I was Brooke, I'd do it." I shrugged my shoulders and instantly hated that I said that out loud when Jase's skin fell away from mine.

"Yeah. No." Tucker chuckled. "I'd kick Liam's ass."

"For fucking your sister?" I narrowed my eyes at him. "Your grown-ass sister?"

Jase shifted in his seat next to me.

"Of course. He's my friend not some..." He waved his hand in the air trying to come up with a word.

"A what?" I asked as my blood started to boil. "What would you prefer, I fuck a stranger? A guy off Tinder? Maybe a local rock star I heard playing at the bar?"

Tucker rolled his eyes. "You know what I mean."

"No." I shook my head. "I don't."

Jase's knee nudged mine again, this time it was a warning to calm down, but I didn't care.

"You're telling me that you'd prefer for me to go home

with our waiter than for me to fuck Jase." I hiked my thumb in Jase's direction.

"Well, Jase is your boss."

"And he's hot," I challenged.

My brother stared me down, and our food arrived at that exact moment. Neither one of us spoke, but Kennedy breathed out a "Oh, thank God."

I looked up at the waiter then. He was cute, not really my type, but I could do a lot worse. I found his name on the little name tag on his left chest. *Alex.*

"Hey, Alex."

He looked up at me as he set down the last of our food.

"Are you single?"

His eyes jumped to Jase, I'm assuming because he was sitting right next to me.

"Don't worry about him." I waved in Jase's direction. "I'm not allowed to fuck him."

"Dear God." This time it was Jase who spoke.

"I am." Alex looked a bit scared as he answered.

"Me too." I leaned a bit closer to him on my elbow. "I'll leave my number on the table." I tapped against the wood. "Use it."

A soft blush glowed on his cheeks, and I found it endearing. Jase didn't blush. I wasn't even sure he was capable of being embarrassed.

Alex smiled and moved away from our table. I turned my head and smiled at my brother.

"You are the biggest brat I've ever met." He rolled his eyes at me.

"And you're ridiculous." I stabbed my fork into my food. "If I want to fuck Jase, I'll fuck Jase."

"And wreck your career and probably your friendship." He motioned between the two of us.

I leaned in closer so the other tables couldn't overhear me. "Probably my lady bits too."

Kennedy burst out in laughter then and a bit of my anger disappeared.

She looked around the table before taking a giant bite of her pasta. "This is going to be a fun week."

CHAPTER 18
JASE

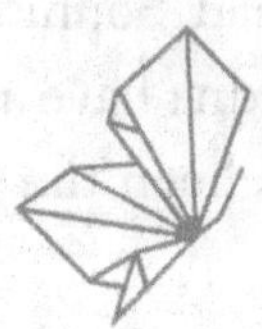

I haven't seen Sophie since dinner last night.

I wanted her to come back to my house with me. I was prepared to beg her, but Kennedy hopped in her car and she barely glanced my way as they headed back toward her parents' house.

Tucker had blown off what she said about fucking me within minutes after the conversation, but I knew that I needed to tell him. No matter what came out of this, I couldn't keep this secret behind his back.

I didn't want him to take it out on her.

If he was going to find out, it was going to be from me. I could take his anger on me if that was what he needed to do.

His bachelor party was tonight. Sophie and I had to make it through this last day of work before we were off for five days, and I hated that I wasn't going to be with her again tonight.

But it would be my perfect opportunity to talk to Tucker.

I had already heard three different presentations this morning, and I was beyond over it. Only one of them was truly worth presenting to the Anderson Development team, and even then, I was worried that our competition had something better.

If I had kept my head down over the last few weeks and worked, I would have my own plans as a backup, but I didn't have shit.

That wasn't true. I had Sophie, at least what she was willing to give me, but I didn't have anything for work.

Work that has always been the most important thing in my life.

Tom's team was up next, and even though he was an asshole, I was hopeful that their plans would blow everyone else's out of the water.

Tom walked in with Sean, Darren, and Sophie behind him. Sophie waved at Mr. Norman as she took a seat, and he grinned at her. She didn't look at me.

Tom handed Mr. Norman and me each a folder that contained their plans. I opened it and flipped through the pages as he started to talk. It was good, really good actually. Tom had obviously spent a lot of hours going over every detail, making sure every code was accounted for.

Mr. Norman noticed too.

"This is good, Tom." He nodded down at the folder in front of him. "The best we've seen."

We were supposed to be announcing the plans we'd present with the entire company, but Mr. Norman wasn't a bullshitter.

Tom nodded but didn't say thank you.

"There may be a few things that we might need to shift." Mr. Norman flipped the page and looked over the next section. "But it's good."

Sean and Darren were smiling at each other. I don't

know who actually drew up these plans or if they had done them together, but if we picked their plans, their entire team would benefit. It would be their project. Their baby.

"If you have the time, I actually have a second set of plans I think you should look at." Tom pulled out another folder and handed it to us.

His team members looked at each other and clearly had no clue what was going on. Apparently, they weren't privy to this information.

Mr. Norman opened the folder between us, and I instantly recognized the plans from Sophie's apartment.

Mr. Norman quickly flipped through the folder and his eyes lit up as he took in page after page. My gaze flew up to Sophie, but she was staring down at the folder with her lip between her teeth.

She didn't know Tom was going to be showing her plans. Hell, I'm not even sure how he got his hands on them. The last I knew, she wasn't planning on showing them to anyone.

"These are..." Mr. Norman looked up at Tom. "These are exceptional. Why didn't you show me these first?"

Tom looked over at Sophie, but she was still staring down at the folder in Mr. Norman's hand. "These are Sophie's plans."

Sophie's gaze finally snapped up then.

"I dismissed them at first because she's new and she told me these were just practice, but I finally took a look at them this morning."

Sophie looked like she was in shock, and I didn't blame her. Tom was a dick ninety percent of the time. For him to do this, he had to be impressed.

And he should be.

"Sophie." Mr. Norman leaned back in his chair. "These are incredible."

"Thank you." She mumbled the words like she was in a daze.

"Well, Tom." Mr. Norman looked back to him. "Which plans do you think we should go with?"

I think we were all holding our breath for his answer.

"Sophie's. They're unique and efficient. I think her plans will win us the project."

"I agree." It was the first time I had spoken since they entered the room. Sophie's eyes met mine. She looked overwhelmed, and I wanted nothing more than to hold her. To celebrate with her.

"Congratulations, Sophie." Mr. Norman smiled at her. "Now we just have to present your plans to the Anderson Development team."

I watched as she visibly swallowed.

"I don't know what to say." She looked from person to person in the room. "Thank you."

Mr. Norman pulled Sophie into a hug before we finally left the room. I followed Sophie toward her office. I wanted to talk about last night. I wanted to congratulate her about today.

I had no damn clue where her head was at.

I walked into her office behind her, and I slowly closed the door behind me. I pressed my back against the door and opened my mouth to say something, but Sophie surprised me when she whirled toward me and pressed her lips against mine.

"Can you believe this?" Her breath was ragged against my lips.

"I can. I told you in your apartment that they were good. I wasn't lying."

She leaned her head back and I wrapped my arms around her back to keep her standing. "I can't believe Tom showed them."

"I'm with you there. That surprised the shit out of me."

She looked back up at me and she was so unabashedly herself in that moment that I refused to look away. Her cheeks were flushed, her eyes a bit wild, and it hit me when her pink lips fell into a simple smile.

I was falling for her, and that smile on her face, it was the only thing that could possibly matter.

Not her brother.

Not this job.

That smile suddenly mattered more than anything else.

I didn't know when it happened, but it was too late, I was plummeting and there was nothing I could do to stop it.

She wrapped her arms around my neck, and I wondered if she could see it, what I unexpectedly realized must be staring back at her.

She pressed her lips against mine, and I breathed her in as my hands pulled her tighter against me.

"I wish we didn't have these parties tonight," she whispered against my mouth. "I wish it was just us."

"Me too." I kissed the corner of her mouth then against her jaw. "Tomorrow," I promised her.

"You'll be hungover." She laughed and pulled slightly out of my reach. "Plus, I have to help get things ready for the wedding."

I pushed off the door and took a step closer to her. Her smile turned a bit wicked as she tracked my movements.

I was almost to her, ready to throw her against her desk

without giving two fucks if her door was locked or not when a loud buzzing came from her desk. She lifted her cell phone and her gaze hit mine as she answered.

"Hey, Brooke."

She popped the top button of her shirt, and I watched as her fingers trailed over the soft skin of her breast.

"Yeah. I'll be leaving work soon." She looked up at me and closed the distance between us. My mouth was against her chest within seconds.

She nodded her head even though Brooke couldn't see her. "Uh huh," she hummed.

I pressed the heel of my hand against her center. It didn't matter that she was still wearing pants. She pushed forward into my touch and her body begged me for more.

"Right. I got the Jon Snow cutout. It's huge." She squeezed her eyes closed as I added a little more pressure.

I moved behind her and she arched a brow at me over her shoulder before I pulled her back against me. I was perched on the edge of her desk and her ass was pressed against my groin like it was fucking made to be there.

Her breast filled my hand, and her head leaned back against my chest as I rolled her nipple between my fingers.

"Yeah. Pin the ponytail on Khal Drogo. I have it in my trunk."

I laughed, and she elbowed me.

I pressed my hand against her stomach, bringing her body harder against mine, and she stopped her movements. I listened to her hum her agreements as I slid my hand beneath her pants.

The lace of her panties was soft against my fingertips and her breathing became rough against the phone. I didn't dip beneath her panties. Instead, I rubbed the smallest circles over the fabric and watched as she covered her mouth with her hand as the smallest whimper left her lips. She didn't want me to stop though. Her ass was grinding against me in the same pattern of my fingers, and when I sped up so did she.

"I don't." She cleared her throat and her words came out a bit breathless. "I don't think the White Walkers are very sexy. Are we sure we want them at the bachelorette party?"

She listened for a second, and I took the moment to lift my fingers away from her then smack them back down against her. Her ass jerked against me, and I knew she could feel my cock as it strained against my pants.

"Kennedy's so fucking weird." She could barely get the words out. "Okay. Yeah." She nodded her head again. "I'll see you then."

She let her phone fall to the floor with a soft clatter and her body became heavier against mine. I flicked her earlobe with my tongue before I nipped the tender flesh between my teeth.

She turned her face as far as she could. Her lips touched mine as she breathed harder and harder.

"You're bad," she whispered, her words barely there.

"You love it." I pushed my fingers harder against her. She was so fucking wet that I could feel every bit of it through her panties.

"I do." She nodded her head then wrapped a hand around my neck to pull me closer to her.

She kissed me with a desperation that her hips chased against my hand. Her body tightened. She was so fucking close.

I pressed just a little harder, I kissed her just a little deeper, and she fell apart in my hands. Her deep moan disappeared in my mouth, and her hands disappeared in my hair. She was holding me like she never wanted to let go, and I didn't want her to either.

This right here, me and her without any complications, it was perfect. But it was also an illusion.

She would come down off the high I had just given her, and we would still be in her office surrounded by walls that seemed to be closing in on us. We would still have her brother's wedding in a few days, and we would still be putting on a fucking show.

I hated it. This game we were playing. I fucking craved every moment of it, but I hated it just the same.

Her hands loosened in my hair, but my grip didn't budge on her.

I pressed a small kiss at the apex of her shoulder.

When she tried to slide her hand against my cock, I stopped her and shook my head. God, I needed to fuck her, but I couldn't. Not like this. My head was too fucked, and I needed to get my shit together.

"I have to get some work done." I smiled at her.

"I better get going anyway." She finally pulled out of my touch. "Apparently our Game of Thrones bachelorette party needs White Walker penis ice cubes."

I chuckled and tucked a piece of hair behind her ear.

"Brooke?"

"Of course." She shrugged her shoulders. "I don't think she's actually seen the show. She just googled male characters."

"Well, don't have too much fun with those ice penises." I straightened up off her desk and started to pass her.

"You either." She shook her head. "Not with ice penises,

but you know what I mean. At the bachelor party." She bit down on her bottom lip.

"I won't." I smirked at her, but she actually looked a bit concerned.

"If I text you while I'm at the bachelor party, will that be too much?"

She grinned and shook her head. "Absolutely not."

"Be careful." I chuckled and pressed a kiss to the tip of her nose.

"Aye aye, boss man." She saluted me, and I rolled my eyes. "It's not as easy to fall off a bar as you would think."

"Dear God." I walked out of her office with the sound of her laughter trailing me.

CHAPTER 19
SOPHIE

The hotel suite looked like there was a *Game of Thrones* battle in here. There was stuff everywhere. I thought that I was a bit over the top, but Brooke, she took the cake.

But she knew Kennedy so well.

Kennedy screamed when she walked in. Actually screamed. She noticed every little detail as she walked around the room with Brooke's hand in hers, and apparently, she thought the White Walker ice penises were the best thing in the world.

They were actually a huge hit. Pun intended.

I handed Kennedy a shot, and she wrapped me in her arms before we toasted.

Brooke looked around the room at Kennedy, me, and a few other girls who had traveled to Tennessee for Kennedy's wedding that I didn't know.

"The first rule of the bachelorette party is that Kennedy must have a drink in her hand at all times."

Kennedy rolled her eyes, but Brooke continued.

"The second rule of the bachelorette party is that you

must complete all the tasks on your scavenger hunt." She handed each of us a small card, and I quickly skimmed over the tasks numbered one through ten.

1. Get a piggyback ride from a guy. 2 points.
2. Get a condom from a guy. 1 point.
3. Get a picture with a guy who has a mullet. 1 point.
4. Get a picture with a police officer. 1 point.
5. Get a guy to give the bachelorette a lap dance. 2 points.
6. Get carried into the bar. 2 points.
7. Get a stranger to write down sexual advice for the bachelorette. 2 points.
8. Bring home something blue. 1 point.
9. Smooch a stranger. 3 points.
10. Dance on the bar. 3 points.

"Are you serious?" Kennedy was staring down at her list.

"Yes, ma'am." Brooke held her shot in the air, and slowly one by one, we each joined her. "To Kennedy."

"To Kennedy." We each joined in then downed our shots.

"Now let's pin this ponytail on Khal Drogo and get you bitches drunk."

Kennedy laughed, and Brooke slid another drink in her hand.

...

We had just gotten to the bar, and I'm pretty sure ninety percent of us were already well on our way to being beyond tipsy. Kennedy was laughing hysterically at things that were barely even funny, and I watched Brooke shove a bottle of water in her hand on the ride over.

We all climbed out of the Uber and started toward the bar. There were three guys leaning against the wall smoking, and the one in the center was watching me as the smoke slipped past his lips.

I made my way toward him and tucked my hands in my back pockets. My jeans were tight, and I knew he noticed when his eyes didn't move off them.

"Hi."

His gaze snapped up to mine and he took another drag of his cigarette.

"Hi, darlin'."

His voice was rough and insanely sexy, but it didn't do a damn thing for me. Instead, all I could think about was how dull his eyes looked compared to Jase's and how his smirk did nothing to my lady parts.

"I know this is a weird request." I looked behind me, and Brooke was grinning as she led Kennedy toward the door. "You think you can give me a piggyback ride into the bar?"

He dropped his cigarette to the ground and smashed it with his boot. "Bachelorette party?" He cocked an eyebrow.

"You give a lot of piggyback rides around here?"

"No." He shook his head a lot. "But I end up giving away a lot of condoms."

I pulled my scavenger hunt out of my pocket and tapped against it. "If you have an extra, I could take one of those too."

He chuckled and pulled his wallet out of his back pocket. He held the condom out to me between two fingers, and my fingers grazed his as I reached out for it. I tucked it in my pocket, and he turned his back to me.

"Hop on." He reached his hands out behind him to grab my legs, and I didn't hesitate as I clumsily jumped onto his back and wrapped my heeled feet around his waist.

His hands tightened around my thighs as he started moving toward the bar, and for half a second, all I could think about was how wrong his touch felt.

His buddies chuckled as he carried me into the bar, and I gave them a quick wave of my fingers. Tonight was supposed to be fun. The last thing I needed to do all night was worry about Jase, what he was doing, or my nonexistent relationship with him.

The girls cheered as I finally made it into the bar, and my chariot set me down on the ground. I patted his chest in thanks, and he gave me a quick wink before heading to the bar.

"That was a five-point deal." I curtsied in front of the girls and held out the condom. "Piggyback, carried in the bar, and a condom. You girls better get busy."

They laughed, and Brooke handed me a drink. I took a sip and sat down next to Kennedy.

"Are you excited?" I bumped my shoulder into hers.

She looked over at me like a lovesick fool. "More than you know."

"And you're sure about Tucker?" I arched an eyebrow at her. "He can be a bit of an ass you know."

She wrapped her arm around mine just as my phone vibrated in my pocket. "He's only like that because he loves you."

"I know." I looked around the bar. "But he's going to

have to get over it eventually. I can't be a hermit who lives with her parents forever."

She snorted and took another sip of her drink. I pulled my phone out of my pocket and looked down at the screen. There on my screen was a selfie of Jase with him rolling his eyes.

Jase: Is this over yet? Ryan is telling stories about our high school days.

I chuckled and held up my phone to snap a photo. Ryan was Jase and Tucker's other best friend during high school, and he was nothing more than a damn jokester.

I took a quick photo and started typing.

Me: I just got a piggyback ride so it's not so bad.

"Who is that for?" Kennedy's voice almost made me jump out of my skin.

"No one." I shook my head and flipped my phone over.

"Okay." She poked me in my side. "Keep your secret boyfriend to yourself. Wait." She gasped and her mouth popped open.

I held my breath.

"Are you bringing a Tinder date to our wedding?"

"What?" I shoved her arm. "You're ridiculous."

"True." She took another drink. "But could you imagine your brother's face if you showed up with some random hottie? How about piggyback boy?" She pointed her finger in the direction toward the bar, and I followed her gaze to where he was still watching us.

"That's not happening." I looked back toward her and tried to avoid looking his way again. I didn't need him thinking that the piggyback ride was some grand opening for him to get into my pants.

"We'll find you someone." She started looking around the bar, but Brooke grabbed her hands and started pulling her to the dance floor.

"Come on, Sophie," she yelled over the music.

I lifted my drink and took another sip. "I'll be right there."

When she was finally distracted, I checked my phone again.

Jase: Wait. Who gave you a piggyback ride?

I laughed and snapped a photo of our scavenger hunt game.

It took him a few minutes before he replied.

Jase: You have to kiss a stranger?

Sophie: Have to is relative. If I want the 3 points, I do.

His next response was almost immediate.

Jase: Don't.

My heart started racing at his one-word text. Did he not want me to kiss someone else because I was fucking him? Or did he just not want me to kiss anyone else?

Those were two very different things, and I wasn't sure how I felt about either of them. We had never discussed being exclusive when it came to our sex life, but I also hadn't put much thought into the fact that he could have been fucking someone else this whole time.

Just the thought alone makes my chest ache in a way that I hate.

But if Jase didn't want me to kiss someone else just because? That was different. That made my heart race and my hands sweat. I knew that I didn't want him to kiss anyone else. But I also knew that I promised myself I wouldn't fall for Jase Hale again.

It was impossible.

Me and him.

We were never meant to be.

Sophie: Is that an order?

His next answer came in a series of texts as I held my breath.

Jase: No.

Jase: But I don't want you to.

Jase: Unless that's what you want.

Jase: Is that what you want?

I could lie to him. If I was smart, I would have, but I couldn't. No matter how many times my fingers bounced over the letters, I couldn't press them.

Sophie: No.

Jase: Good.

Jase: You look gorgeous by the way.

Jase: Send me another picture so I can get
the image of you kissing someone else out
of my brain.

I smiled and pushed out my chair to walk to the bathroom. I almost hit Brooke with the door as I moved inside.

"Where's Kennedy?" I looked around the small bathroom.

"Dancing. Are you going to join us?" She dried her hands on a paper towel.

"Yeah." I nodded my head. "Let me pee, and I'll be out there."

"Alright." She dropped the paper towel in the trash. "Hurry up."

I dashed into the bathroom stall, and I didn't think twice as I pulled the edge of my tank top down enough so my black lace bra was in full view. I leaned my back against the door and snapped a photo.

I lifted my shirt and hit send before I really looked at the photo. I looked hot. My breasts were on full display for him, but it wasn't that. My eyes were a bit glazed from the alcohol, my skin a bit flushed from talking to Jase, and my lips were still a perfect shade of red that I painted on before we left the hotel.

I tucked my phone back in my pocket and pushed out the door. It was time to dance with my girls.

CHAPTER 20

JASE

My jaw hurt like a bitch.

It didn't matter how much liquor was coursing through my veins. It wasn't enough to mask my best friend's fist against my jaw.

I guess I deserved it though. Telling him about his sister while he was drinking was probably the worst idea I ever had.

But they wouldn't fucking leave me alone. My jackass friends wanted to know who I was texting. They wanted to know who was keeping my mind preoccupied.

When I told him it was his sister, he stared at me for a moment before his fist landed against my face. Liam pulled him off just as quickly, but it didn't matter, he had already gotten in his hit. I had almost made it the entire night without opening my mouth. We were back at my house, and we were all drunk. I couldn't take it anymore. The fucking secret was eating me alive.

"Why her?" he yelled from Liam's arms.

"Are you kidding me, man?" I rubbed my hand over my

jaw and tasted the blood that trickled from my bottom lip. "She's not a fucking child."

"No." He jerked his arms out of Liam's hold and moved toward me. "But she is my fucking sister. You should have told me."

"I am telling you."

He shook his head. "This doesn't count." He pointed his finger at me. "You should have told me when you started fucking my sister."

I ran my fingers through my hair. "What did you want me to do? Call you once she pulled down her skirt and say 'Hey, man.'"

Tucker jumped toward me again, but Liam caught him this time.

"Jase, you idiot."

I didn't care what Liam had to say though.

"It's not your fucking business." I held my arms out wide. "Do you really think I'm going to hurt her? Do you really think I'm that guy?"

"You've been that guy before," Tucker spit at me.

"So have you," I countered.

That seemed to sober him a bit. "So, what is it? Just sex?"

"I don't know," I growled in frustration.

"What do you mean you don't know?" He was getting irritated again.

"It's not just sex to me."

"Oh shit." I wasn't sure if that came from Liam or Ryan.

"So, what? You're in love with my sister?" Tucker narrowed his eyes at me.

My heart raced more than when he hit me.

"If I am?" I sat back down and stared at him.

"What does Sophie think?" When I didn't answer, he laughed. "She doesn't know."

I leaned my head back against the chair. "Are you going to hit me again? I'd like to go ahead and get it out of the way if you are."

"No." Tucker shook his head and lifted his drink to his lips. "This is better."

I looked back up at him. "What's better?"

"Watching you be lovesick over my sister." He smirked, and Ryan started laughing.

"I'm fucked, aren't I?"

"Completely." Tucker slapped his hand against my shoulder then nodded toward the kitchen. "Now let's go take another shot before I pass out."

I followed him and picked up the shot he handed me. He held up his shot and tapped it against mine. "Don't fucking hurt her."

...

Tucker was passed out facedown on my guest bed with Ryan right next to him. It took almost every bit of strength that Liam and I had to get his drunk ass in there. Liam face-planted on the couch once we finally got him in there and set the empty glasses in my sink before hitting the lights and dragging my own ass to bed.

I clicked on my phone and stared down at my text. I had messaged Sophie about thirty minutes ago to make sure they made it back to their hotel. She still hadn't answered me.

I knew she was probably passed out in bed by now, but I still had the urge to call her just to be sure.

I clicked back through our texts through the night and

opened the last photo she sent me. She was so fucking hot, and the irrational part of me hated that other men got to see her like that tonight. Obviously, she had her shirt pulled down just for me, or at least I hoped, but it wasn't even her tits that made her so exceptional.

Don't get me wrong. Her tits were fucking perfection, but it was more than that. It was the way her bottom lip was just a bit heavier than her top one. It was the way a dimple formed on only her right cheek when she laughed at something that was really funny.

That dip at the base of her neck where her collarbones began.

That spark in her eye that reminded me of a brewing storm.

Then there were her tits and her perfect damn body.

She was too good for me. She was too good for anyone.

It didn't stop me though as I grabbed my cock in my hand and stared at her through my phone screen. I could practically smell the soft scent of her skin and the way her hands always clung to my skin as I made her fall apart. My hand moved against me, and I imagined it was hers.

It was almost embarrassing how quickly I could come thinking about her. I was almost there, just a few more short strokes when something hit my bedroom window.

I threw my phone down and jumped out of bed. My hand had just wrapped around the bat that I kept hidden just behind my headboard when something hit my window again followed by a giggle.

Someone started shhing and more giggling ensued.

I pulled open my curtains and stared out my window at Sophie, Kennedy, and Brooke. Brooke looked like she was the only one who didn't need to lean against the house to stay standing on her feet when I opened the window.

Sophie picked up another stick, almost falling over, before aiming it back at my window. She threw it with a giggle on her lips, and it almost hit me in the head.

"What the hell are you all doing?"

She shrieked as if she didn't realize I was standing in the open window then started laughing again.

"This one." Brooke hiked her thumb in Sophie's direction while her other arm held onto Kennedy. "Won't shut up about you." She looked back at Kennedy. "This one won't go to bed because she misses Tucker."

I smiled at the goofy smile on Sophie's face. She was far too drunk to be embarrassed.

"Why are you all at my window?" I clarified my question.

"Because she misses you and she says her brother will kill her for missing you." She shrugged her shoulders as if that was the easiest explanation ever.

"I'll be right there."

I turned my back to my window and smiled at the three of them dying in laughter. I flipped on the outside light and made my way out the front door to help Brooke.

She was still holding onto Kennedy when I got out there, but Sophie was gone.

"Where..." I started my question, but Brooke pointed to my bedroom window just as Sophie's laughter echoed through.

I rolled my eyes with a laugh before I took Kennedy out of Brooke's hold and lifted her in my arms.

"You're so handsome." Kennedy laughed and was complete dead weight in my arms.

"You better not let your future husband hear you say that. He might kick my ass."

She looked up at me. "Yeah, right. He'd never."

"Oh yeah?" I ran my tongue over my split bottom lip.

She jolted in my arms and Brooke chuckled beside me.

"He hit you?" Kennedy sounded a mix of shocked, mad, and maybe a little impressed.

"He did." I nodded my head and moved us through the front door.

"That's hot." She leaned her head back and looked around the room upside down.

I shook my head at her and carried her into my guest room. Tucker was dead center in the bed on his back, and Ryan had been shoved to the tiniest sliver of mattress on the side. I plopped Kennedy down on the mattress beside Tucker, and he wrapped his arm around her as soon as her body pressed against his.

I left the drunken lovebirds and Ryan alone and slowly closed the door behind me. I peeked into the living room to check on Brooke, but she had already squeezed herself on the couch with Liam. Her leg was across him and his arm was wrapped around her back holding her to him. I didn't know what was going on there, but I wasn't touching it with a ten-foot pole.

Instead, I flipped off the outside light and made my way back into my bedroom. Sophie was facedown on my bed wearing nothing but a black bra and the tiniest pair of black panties I had ever seen, and the softest little snore echoed throughout my room.

I shut the window then climbed under the blanket pulling Sophie along with me. She wrapped her body around mine and pressed her face into my neck.

"You smell good." Her words were so mumbled that I almost couldn't make them out, but she snuggled closer to me and took a deep breath against my skin.

"You smell like vodka." I laughed and pushed her hair over her shoulder.

"I may have drunk a bit." She held up her thumb and finger about an inch apart.

"A bit, huh?" I ran my hand down her back, and she shivered under my touch.

She leaned back to look up at me. "Okay, maybe a bit more than a bit." She grinned then her smile dropped, and her hand lifted to touch my lip. "What happened?"

She started to sit up, but I pulled her back down against me. "It's nothing."

"It doesn't look like nothing." She frowned.

"Okay. It's a bit more than nothing."

She didn't smile like I had expected her to. Instead, she searched my eyes. "Who did this?"

"I deserved it." I tried to press my lips to hers, but she pulled back.

"That's not what I asked."

I huffed and ran my fingers through my hair. "Tucker."

She pushed off me and stared down at me in shock. "You told him."

I nodded my head. "I couldn't lie to him anymore."

"And he hit you?"

I rubbed my still aching jaw. "He has one hell of a right hook too."

She looked to the door like she had half a mind to march out of my room wearing nothing more than her underwear and confronting her brother. I leaned up on my elbow and reached out to turn her face back toward me.

"It's fine. We're cool."

She narrowed her eyes at me. "My brother is cool with the fact that we're fucking each other."

And with the fact that I'm falling in love with you.

"Technically." I pulled her back over my chest. "I haven't fucked you in like three days. I'm starting to have withdrawals."

"Oh yeah." She grinned and ran her finger over an old scar on my jaw absently.

"Yeah." I pressed my groin against her before flipping us over and settling my body on top of hers.

Her hair was a wild mess around her and her smile was addictive. "I think you may be getting a little too attached there, Mr. Hale."

She was playing, but her words hit home.

I was beyond a little too attached.

"Well." I shrugged. "I better get another taste just to make sure."

She laughed, and I ran my nose down her neck to just between her breasts. Her chest rose just slightly to meet my mouth. She wanted it just as badly as I did. She was just as addicted as I was.

I pushed the thin fabric down just below her nipple, and I stared up at her as I pressed the tip of my tongue against her flesh. She bit her bottom lip as she watched me, making my cock impossibly hard.

I ripped her bra down her chest, the fabric pushing her breasts higher, and I reached behind her and fumbled with the clasp as I ran my teeth over the underside of her breast.

I felt like I was spiraling out of control.

I had taken off more bras in my life than I could count, but I was too eager to touch, too impatient to have my mouth on her, and I was fumbling around like a boy who had just seen his first set of tits.

"Jase." She moaned my name and her bra finally fell away from her body.

I kissed down her body making sure to taste every inch of skin. She squirmed under me, particularly so when my teeth skimmed over her ribs and her hip bones.

"Please," she begged and thrust her hips up against me.

"What do you want, Sophie?" I breathed the words against her panties.

She writhed against my mouth. Her body begging me for something she didn't want to say out loud. Her thumb glided into the waistband of her panties and she tried to force her hips up underneath me to pull them down.

I let my mouth follow the path of her hand.

But it wasn't where she wanted me.

She tried to force my head where she wanted me, but I only laughed against her skin. "Use your words, Soph."

She growled in frustration. "I want you."

"Where?" I kissed the inside of her thigh.

"Everywhere. I just..." She moaned as I pressed my lips right at the apex of her thighs. "I need you."

I dove into her flesh, and she threw her head back with that fucking lip still between her teeth. I pushed her thighs open as far as they would go, and she helped me. There wasn't anything between us, at least when it came to our bodies, but I still wanted more.

Her body shuddered under my tongue faster than she had ever come to this point before, and I let the pressure off just slightly as she tried to force me to give her more. I moved up her body, my mouth nipping at any skin as I passed, and I lined my cock up against her.

I needed to feel her. I needed her to fall apart with me inside her.

She wrapped her legs around my waist as I pushed into her, and she used my body as leverage to lift her own hips to meet mine. She was desperate beneath me. Her body so reactive to every little touch of skin.

For a second, I wondered if she was this reactive with everyone, but I forced the thought from my mind. I had enough adrenaline running through my veins already. I didn't need the added rage of wanting to kill every mother-fucker who had ever touched her before.

I pushed her knees apart and rolled my hips as I searched her face. I needed to see her eyes, and I needed to look at her to calm my racing heart. But she wasn't looking at me. Her head was turned to the side, and she gripped the sheets in her hands as she mewled and arched her back off the bed.

She tried to slam her hips against mine, but I stopped her. I forced her hips to the bed with one hand as I took my time discovering every inch of her. Her body was tightening around me, and I knew that she was so damn close again already.

It would take nothing to push her over the edge.

But I wasn't ready.

I needed her to look at me.

"Sophie." I breathed her name causing her to moan and push her hips harder against mine. "Baby, look at me."

This time she finally did. She blinked her eyes open, and there was a wild defiance in them. She was unwilling to break, and there was something about me that made her fear the uncertainty. But I didn't want to break her. That one simple look, that taste of her wildness, I felt intoxicated on the wild crushing beauty that she seemed to hide behind her precious defenses.

It was like truly feeling gravity for the first time, the pull more intense than anything I had ever felt before, and when she cried out my name as her body finally fell apart, I knew that Sophie Moore had the power to destroy me.

And there wasn't a damn thing I could do about it.

CHAPTER 21
SOPHIE

My head was pounding.

When I woke up this morning, I was engulfed in Jase's heat and an anxiety that didn't seem to be going away with my drunkenness. Last night was too much.

I was too drunk. Jase made me feel too much, and I was overwhelmed.

I didn't know what to think.

I knew that last night was more than the alcohol. But I couldn't let my head get clouded over amazing sex. Even if I came harder staring into Jase's eyes than I ever had before.

It was still sex.

"Morning." Jase looked up at me as I snapped my bra back into place.

"Morning." I smiled at him then threw my shirt over my head. I had no damn clue where I managed to lose my pants.

"Where are you going?" His voice was so damn gravelly in the morning, and I had to remind myself why I was looking for my pants in the first place.

He tucked an arm under his pillow and bunched it

under his head. He was watching my every movement, and for the first time in as long as I could remember, I felt unsure of myself in Jase's presence.

"The wedding's tomorrow. Remember?" I spotted my jeans across the room and hurried over and pulled them up my legs. "If I don't get Kennedy to my mom's house for all the wedding stuff, my mom will kill me."

"Come here." He patted the bed next to him.

I grabbed my heels and dropped down next to his hand. I leaned forward to put my painful-ass heels back on my feet when his arm wrapped around my stomach, and he pulled me back into him.

"What are you doing?" I chuckled and hoped I didn't sound as panicked as I felt. "Did you not hear what I said?"

"I heard you." He leaned over me, his bare chest barely touching mine. "But I don't care."

I scoffed and tried to push myself back off his bed. He caught my hands in his and pinned them above my head.

"Jase, I'm serious." I blew a piece of hair out of my face.

"So am I." He ran his nose up my neck. "You're not running out of my room in a hurry without kissing me."

"What if I don't want to kiss you?" I countered, but we both knew it was a lie.

"You do." He pressed his lips against the corner of my mouth, and I had to fight the urge to turn my face and kiss him. I wanted to, desperately, but I also wanted to prove the cocky asshole wrong.

"Kiss me, Soph." His words vibrated against my lips, and I swear, that man had discovered every possible way to get under my skin.

I searched his eyes as I spoke. "I'm only doing this because I'm in a hurry and don't have time to fight you."

"Oh. Of course." I felt more than saw his lips form a smile.

He didn't kiss me. He was going to make me be the one to do it, and even though I hated giving in to him, my desperation to prove to myself that nothing had changed after last night was too strong.

Pinned against the bed, I raised my mouth to his, lips parted, breathing heavy, and I kissed him. The curl of his fingertips against my hands was gentle but seemed to wrap around me harder than I had ever felt before. It didn't matter how many times he had ripped the clothes from my body and devoured my skin, this kiss felt more intimate than all those times combined.

My bones ached with the urge to run. I knew he was sure to ruin me, to shatter my heart, but I couldn't pull away from him. My hands shook beneath his, but his hold was fragile, and his kiss was merciless. There wasn't a part of me that he left untouched.

My fingers tightened around his, and my chest heaved as I attempted to catch my breath.

It was a collection of moments hitting me all at once as I tried to force logical thought into my brain. It was impossible.

He was surrounding me, his lips still devouring mine, and nothing about us was logical.

My heart was betraying me. I could feel it. Like a half-remembered dream, the memory of my infatuation with Jase was a series of hazy details, and they all paled in comparison to what I felt now. It was uncomfortable and made me feel restless in my skin. It was a soft murmur in the back of my mind, and as soon as I heard it, I knew that it would drive me mad with the truth I was desperately trying to avoid.

I was in love with Jase Hale, and it was devastating to remember that we were never meant to be.

A loud pounding came from Jase's bedroom door, and I jumped in shock of both the sound and my own realization.

"Wake up, sleepyheads," Kennedy's voice called through the door. "Your mom is already calling."

I pushed out from under Jase's touch and quickly threw on my shoes. Jase was smiling as he climbed out of bed completely naked, and although the view was enough to take my breath away, it was that sleepy, satisfied smile that I tried to commit to memory.

He threw on a pair of sweats, low on his hips, and I threw open the door as soon as he had himself covered. My brother was standing in the kitchen with a coffee cup pressed to his mouth, but I didn't have the time or energy to deal with him this morning. Instead, I avoided looking at him and found Kennedy in the bathroom brushing her teeth with her finger.

"You ready?" I ran my fingers through my hair and tied it in a knot at the top of my head.

"Yeah." She nodded her head before spitting toothpaste into the sink. "Your mom said they already delivered the tables and chairs this morning."

She had a wild look in her eye, a nervousness I rarely saw in her anymore.

I wondered if she saw the same look reflected back at her.

"Let's go get us a wedding ready then."

She smiled at me then and wiped her mouth on the back of her hand.

"Holy shit." A laugh bubbled out of her as she grabbed

my hand, and we headed back toward the living room to find Brooke.

Jase wrapped his arm around my stomach as I started to pass him, and right there in front of my brother, without a single fucking care, he kissed me as if it was the most natural thing to do.

Kennedy whistled as Jase loosened his grip on me, but I refused to look her way.

"I'll see you later." Jase spoke low enough for only me to hear.

"Okay." I nodded my head and tried to think clearly.

"Have fun." His hand came down on my ass, and he chuckled as I walked out of his house with a shocked look on my face.

...

My mom was literally the best. She decorated our house for any trivial holiday, and she taught us to have dance parties in the kitchen on a random Wednesday night just because we could.

But getting ready for my brother's wedding?

She had lost her damn mind.

"Sophie." She pointed to a stack of napkins on the dining room table. "Those all need to be folded."

I saluted her considering my fingers were still bleeding from helping her with all the flower arrangements. A bit dramatic, sure, but there were white roses in the mix of sunflowers and anemones and they had thorns.

I had just started folding exactly liked my mother showed me when my phone rang. I didn't recognize the number, and I dismissed it at first until I realized the area code was from Seattle.

I grabbed my phone, almost dropping it on the ground. "Hello."

"May I speak with Ms. Moore?"

"This is she." I ran to my parents' room to get away from the bustle of getting ready for the wedding.

"Hi, Ms. Moore. This is Eric Keller from Keller Architecture and Design."

"Yes. Of course. It's so nice to hear from you, Mr. Keller." I straightened out my shirt even though he couldn't see me.

"Sorry it has taken so long. We had several applicants for the associate architect position at our company, and we wanted to make sure we found the right fit."

My throat was so dry that I could barely speak. "Of course."

"If you're still interested, we'd like to offer you the position." There was a bunch of noise behind him, and I knew that he was probably in his busy office that I had dreamed of working in.

"I don't know what to say." I think I was in shock. I wanted this. More than I had ever wanted anything. I would be out of my parents' house, living in my dream city, working my dream job, and the only thing that was crossing my mind at that moment was Jase.

The urge to tell him yes that I absolutely accepted the position was overwhelming, but the only word that wanted to escape from my lips was no.

"It's a great opportunity," Mr. Keller spoke again. "You beat out some very experienced architects for this position, but you impressed us."

"I…" I started to speak but hesitated. "Do you need an answer today?"

"No." His voice had a bit of an edge to it. "I'll have my assistant send over all the details. Pay, relocation reimbursement, benefits, that sort of thing. If you could give us an answer by the beginning of next week…"

"Absolutely." I sat down on my parents' bed and my knee was bouncing so hard my teeth mashed together. "I'll have an answer for you by Monday."

"Alright. We'll talk to you then."

"Thank you, Mr. Keller." I meant it too. Applying for this position was a long shot. I never expected to actually get it.

"You're welcome. Have a good rest of your week."

"You too."

He hung up the phone before I could manage to say goodbye, but I didn't care.

I stared down at the phone in my hands, and I told myself that I was crazy. I should have already said yes. There was nothing to think about, not one damn thing to consider. Yes. I would be moving away from my parents, but I would visit just like Tucker did.

My parents would support my decision. I knew they would.

So would Tucker.

But my family wasn't making me hesitate.

Jase gave me an opportunity at Norman Architecture when I didn't have any other. And Mr. Norman? He chose my design for the Anderson Development.

I would never get an opportunity like that at Keller Architecture and Design. Not until I had years of work under my belt. But the kind of work they did was exceptional. It was why I had applied there in the first place.

But Jase.

I knew that he shouldn't have even been a factor in my decision. We were fucking for crying out loud. A girl wasn't supposed to make major life decisions based on the man who was giving her orgasms every night.

It was stupid.

But the idea of leaving him scared me far more than the idea of losing this opportunity.

My parents' bedroom door opened, and I jumped as if I had been caught doing something wrong.

"There you are." My brother closed the door behind him.

"Mom is looking everywhere for you."

"Shit." I waved my phone in the air before tucking it in my pocket. "I had a call."

"Jase?" He cocked a brow.

"No, ass. It was from this company in Seattle."

"The job you applied for?" My brother took a step toward me, and I nodded. "What did they say?"

"They offered me the position." I shrugged my shoulders like it was no big deal.

"Holy shit." Tucker closed the distance between us and lifted me in the air. I could barely breathe as he spun me in place. "Congratulations, Soph." He placed me on my feet and kissed the top of my head.

"Thank you." The words sounded weak even to my ears.

"So, what's the problem?"

"There is no problem." I smiled up at him. My brother punched Jase in the face last night when he found out that we were sleeping together. The last thing I needed to do was tell him that I was considering giving up the biggest opportunity that has ever come my way for that same guy. "I'm still hungover."

"Me too." He rubbed his stomach. "That's why I brought tacos."

"For me too?" I became far too excited at the mention of Mexican food.

"Of course." He wrapped his arm around my shoulders. "Let's go."

CHAPTER 22
JASE

This was one of the worst ideas I ever had.

I didn't even know how Sophie felt about me. Hell, I hadn't uttered a single word to her about the way I felt, but I knew. Sex wasn't like that between two people who didn't have feelings for each other.

It was never just sex with her.

I wanted more.

This could all backfire in my face. I could be reading her all wrong. It wouldn't be the first time, but I knew that if I didn't take a chance, I would regret it.

I needed to show her how serious I was.

I needed to prove to her that we could do this.

Mrs. Norman answered the door when I knocked, and she smiled up at me like it was the greatest surprise ever that I had dropped by.

"What are you doing here?" She looked back into the house. "Dan didn't tell me you were coming by. I would have cooked you something."

I smiled and rubbed the back of my neck. "Umm. He actually doesn't know. I'm just dropping by."

Her face sobered a tiny bit. I never just dropped by. "Come on in then." She opened the door just a bit more before calling out for Mr. Norman.

"Hey, Jase." Mr. Norman came around the corner wearing gym shorts and a t-shirt. "I thought you were supposed to be off today."

"I am." I nodded my head and swallowed.

He took a seat at the dining room table and I joined him.

"What's on your mind, son?" He knew that something was off with me. "You aren't quitting, are you?"

"No." I shook my head. "It's nothing like that." At least I hoped it wasn't.

"Well?" He looked as confused as I felt.

"I think I'm in love with Sophie." I tapped my fingers against the table as the corners of his mouth slowly lifted into a smile.

"I owe you twenty dollars," he hollered behind him, and Mrs. Norman came out of the kitchen with two sweet teas in her hands and a shit-eating grin on her face.

"I told you."

"What are you talking about?" I felt like I was trying to swallow my heart.

"Erin called it that first day at lunch. She knew you were in love with her." Mr. Norman chuckled.

I turned my attention to her. "It was the way you looked at her." She shrugged. "It was easy to spot."

"And you didn't think this would be a problem?" I practically screeched at her. "We work together. I'm her boss."

She rolled her eyes, and I swear mine started to bug out of my head.

"Technically, I'm her boss." Mr. Norman leaned back in his chair.

"So, what?" I looked between the two of them. "You don't see a problem with this?"

"It could be problematic, sure." He nodded his head. "But I don't think you're going to break her heart."

"But what if I do?" I voiced the question out loud that had been clouding my damn head since the moment I realized I was falling for her.

"You won't." Mrs. Norman shook her head.

"But I could." I hated to say it out loud, but it was the truth. I was capable of hurting her, and nothing in this world scared me more. I had hurt her before. I never wanted to do it again.

"The fact that you sit here so worried about her and not yourself, tells me that you won't." Mrs. Norman stared straight at me and I couldn't look away. "Have you told her?"

"No."

"Are you going to tell her?" This question came from Mr. Norman.

"I think so." I answered the question as uncertainly as I felt.

"Jase Hale, you better tell that girl."

"I will." I held up my hands when she looked at me like I was lying. "I will. I swear."

"Well, what are you waiting for?"

...

There were people running around everywhere when I got to Sophie's parents' house. Men were carrying tables and chairs and organizing them around the yard where Jojo pointed.

I walked up to her, a bit scared by the way the men jumped at her every word, but she pulled me into a hug as soon as she saw me.

"Where is everyone?" I looked around the yard, but I didn't see anyone that I recognized.

"I sent the girls back to the hotel with Kennedy. We almost have everything set up around here, and the bride needs to relax." A couple guys stood in front of her with a round table, and she pointed them in the right direction. "Tucker and his dad are inside getting the alcohol together."

I pressed a kiss to her cheek and headed in the direction of the boys.

Tucker was unboxing bottles of beers and stuffing them into several different coolers when I walked in, and his dad was leaning against the counter with a cup of coffee in his hands.

"Working hard, Arnie?"

I grabbed the next pack of beers and started handing them to Tucker.

"I've had to put up with that woman for the last six months of wedding planning." He nodded his head out the window in the direction of Jojo. "I deserve a little break."

I laughed and broke down the box before grabbing another.

"Did you hear the good news?" He poured the rest of his coffee in the sink and rinsed his cup.

"Your asshole son managed to convince a woman to actually marry him?"

Tucker shoved me, but his dad laughed. "Other than that."

"No." I shook my head. "What's the good news?"

"Sophie was offered a position at Keller Architecture and Design in Seattle."

My heart stopped at his words. Tucker winced, and I wondered if he didn't plan on telling me. Not that I could be mad at him.

"That's amazing." I barely managed the words.

Keller Architecture and Design was a well-known and well-respected company. He should be proud that his daughter was offered a position. She should be proud.

I was proud of her.

But I was also devastated.

"Dad, you know Jase is her boss. You probably should have let her tell him." Tucker stacked more beers in the cooler and avoided looking me in the eye.

I had just told my best friend in the world that I was in love with his sister last night. The same fucking sister who was leaving.

I hated the look of pity on his face.

"Oh shit." Arnie winced. "I didn't think about that."

"It's fine." I tried to wave his worry away.

"She was just so excited. It's hard not to tell the world." He chuckled, and I opened another pack of beer.

My head started pounding.

"I bet." I laughed and tried to blow off the fact that I was so damn worried about hurting Sophie that I failed to realize I would be the one getting hurt. "She should be ecstatic."

Tucker looked up at me, but this time I avoided him.

"Alright." Tucker stuck the last beer in the cooler and shut the lid. "Let's go see what else Mom has for us to do."

"Yippee." Arnie rolled his eyes but led us out the door.

Tucker put his hand on my chest and blocked my path. "Are you okay?"

I forced a smile. "Of course. Why wouldn't I be?"

"Last night?" He hesitated, but I finished for him.

"We were really drunk." I pushed toward the door again and this time he let his hand drop. "I couldn't be happier for Sophie."

His gaze was filled with doubt, but I refused to take his pity.

Not everyone got their happily ever after. It was never meant for Sophie and me. We were senseless, and our journeys were miles apart.

I just had to make it through the next few days with a smile on my face while trying to be genuinely happy for her.

The two of us were good at keeping secrets. What was one more?

CHAPTER 23
SOPHIE

I was pretty sure Jase looked hotter than I had ever seen him before.

I hadn't laid eyes on him since I left his house after the bachelorette party, and there was something about him that was different.

His hair was cut short, buzzed close to his scalp, and it somehow made his green eyes seem greener and his straight jaw a bit sharper. The black suit he wore was tailored close to his body, a body I knew so well, and I could already imagine all the ladies wiping drool off their face as he walked down the aisle with Brooke on his arm.

He was laughing at something Ryan was saying as I walked up to him. We were moments away from walking down the aisle, and I was anxious for the ceremony to be over so I could be with him.

I was starting to have withdrawals.

"Hey." I saddled up to his side and bumped my arm against his.

He looked down at me, but his face didn't change at all.

"Hey, Sophie." He turned back to Ryan and answered something that they were talking about before I walked up.

He didn't smile down at me like he normally did. There was no signature smirk. Not a single touch of his fingertips.

I was standing beside him like a girl who he had no interest in, and for the first time since we started this, I felt awkward in his presence.

Out of place, out of my league, and completely fucking confused.

I felt like the girl I was when I hated Jase Hale.

Ryan held his hand out to me as the music came on and cued us to take our place. I wrapped my arm around his, my fingers digging into his skin a bit, and I tried to avoid looking at Jase who stood directly behind us with Brooke.

"You look beautiful, Brooke." His words sliced through me, and I held my breath.

"Thank you, Jase."

Of course, Brooke looked beautiful. She was Brooke. My pain had nothing to do with the fact that he had noticed, but he hadn't noticed me.

I stared straight ahead at Liam and Chloe, who had arrived early this morning. Chloe practically ran Tucker and Liam's businesses, and she managed to close the place last night before catching a red-eye to get here this morning. She was a badass, both in personality and looks, even if she was dwarfed by Liam's height.

I let my gaze take in every ounce of ink that covered her skin, and I tried to make out what each and every one was to keep my breathing steady. If I turned around, if I even glanced at him, I knew that I would lose every bit of false bravado I was managing to cling to.

Luckily, the music started, and Liam and Chloe took their first step down the aisle.

"You nervous?" Ryan whispered as we took a step forward to go next.

"A bit." I nodded my head.

He placed his hand over my shaking one on his arm, and I realized that he was mistaking my anger for fear.

Good.

I wouldn't show a reaction to Jase, and I didn't want anyone else to see it either.

We took a step forward when Liam and Chloe hit mid-aisle just as we were instructed, and I reminded myself that today wasn't about me. We were here to celebrate Tucker and Kennedy, and I wouldn't let Jase ruin that.

I wouldn't let him ruin anything.

My brother smiled at me as Ryan led us closer to where he stood, and he looked so damn handsome. I returned his smile and gave him a secret thumbs-up before Ryan went to his side and I took my spot next to Chloe.

I didn't look at Jase as he walked down the aisle with Brooke. Instead, I searched the crowd and waved at different cousins, aunts, and uncles when our gazes met. My mom was sitting in the front row, and she already had a handkerchief against her cheeks.

Brooke took her spot to my left, each of us settling into the spots we were shown, and the music faded before a new song began.

Everyone in the crowd rose as Kennedy and my father appeared. My dad had been shocked when Kennedy asked him to walk her down the aisle, but his yes was immediate and a bit tearful.

None of Kennedy's family was here. Not her parents nor

her brother, and I knew that as much as she hated them, their absence still held a weight over her.

I watched my brother's face as he watched her. There was a moment where it looked like he wasn't breathing.

A breath rushed out of him the closer she got, and I couldn't stop the tear that slipped from my eye when they started to fall from his.

My gaze went from him to Kennedy, but I quickly found myself looking back toward Jase when I noticed that he was staring at me. He looked down when I caught him looking, and I could have sworn there was a touch of anger that crossed his expression.

But Jase didn't do angry.

He was smooth, charismatic, and for as long as I knew him, he rarely cared about something enough to get truly angry.

His signature smirk formed on his face again and he looked back up at me for only a moment.

But whatever he was trying to hide on his face, his eyes couldn't lie. There wasn't an ounce of indifference in his gaze. But he didn't let me look for long, he turned his head to watch Kennedy walk the rest of the way down the aisle, and he didn't risk glancing my direction again.

...

Jase was currently twirling Chloe around the dance floor, and I was pounding slim champagne glasses like a game of flip cup at a frat party.

I was currently on my third glass, and I didn't plan on slowing down.

"What is going on?" Kennedy took a seat next to me, but

I didn't move my attention away from Jase. I didn't give a fuck if he noticed.

I hoped he did.

"Nothing." I smiled and took the last sip of champagne before setting the glass on the table with the rest of my collection.

"Is there a reason you and Jase haven't spoken all day?"

I finally turned my attention to her. "Not that I'm aware of. You'd have to ask him."

Because I would be damned if I did.

I didn't care what his problem was. I was just mad at myself. I promised myself the moment I stepped into Jase's office that I wouldn't let him get the better of me but look at me now.

Movement to my left had me looking over at Chloe as she pulled out the chair, and my gaze searched my parents' yard for Jase just as he walked up behind Kennedy.

"Anyone want a drink?" He looked around the table without ever seeing me.

I held up my hand. "Make it two."

"I think you've had enough." His words were as hard as his stare.

"Oh. I'm sorry. I didn't realize you had a say." I stared back at him with just as much hostility.

"Apparently, I don't." His hands tightened so hard around the back of Kennedy's chair that his knuckles started turning white.

"What's that supposed to mean?" I crossed my legs and sat up straighter.

"Anything you want it to mean, Sophie. That's all that matters, right? What you want?"

"Jase—" Kennedy said his name hesitantly, but I interrupted her.

"What the fuck's your problem, Jase?"

"Are you kidding me?" He narrowed his eyes at me and let out a humorless laugh.

I pushed my ass to the edge of the chair to get a bit closer to him. "What? You told Tucker about us fucking and now you're over it since I'm no longer your dirty little secret."

I heard a gasp, but I didn't care.

I was furious.

"Right." He rubbed his jaw. "I let your brother hit me in my damn face because you were nothing more than that."

He started to walk away, but his fists clenched at his sides and he stormed back toward me. "Speaking of your family." He was barely holding on to his control. "Your dad told me how proud he is of your new job at Keller Architecture and Design."

Fuck.

"Yeah." He nodded his head as if he could see the guilt in my eyes. "I risked my friendship with my best friend for you."

I started to open my mouth, but he spoke again before he could.

"As a matter of fact, I went to our boss's house yesterday. Well, your former boss I guess, and I told him about us. I risked my entire fucking career to tell him about you."

"Jase." I started to stand, but he took a step back.

"Don't fucking '*Jase*' me." He shook his head. "I was willing to give up everything for you. Everything. All while you were walking away."

My brother pulled up to Jase's side and whispered in his

ear. I looked around us then at the crowd that was now watching us, at the display we were putting on.

Jase jerked out of Tucker's grasp and took a step back. He stared at me for a fraction of a moment, but that one look was clear. He was done.

He turned his back to me, and I watched him walk away as I tried to catch my breath.

Kennedy stood and gripped my face in her hands. I didn't even realize I was crying until her hands touched the moisture. "Sophie, I thought you turned the job down."

I nodded my head and took a deep breath. "I did."

CHAPTER 24
JASE

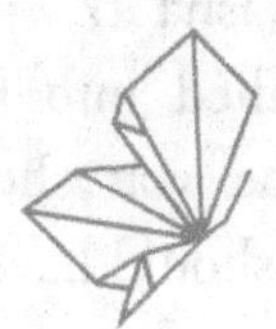

My phone started ringing with Tucker's name before I even made it to the front of the house. I hated myself for what I had just done. This was Tucker and Kennedy's day, and here Sophie and I were ruining everything.

It was pretty fitting actually.

I clicked the fuck-you button and pushed my way to my car. There were cars parked everywhere, but I was pretty sure I could squeeze past them if I really tried.

I just knew that I had to get out of here.

I had to get away from her.

I had already shown too much. It was never part of my plan to let her see how much this shit was affecting me. But I couldn't look her in the face and pretend like I didn't care. We had both done too much of that lately.

I unlocked my car and reached out for the handle just as I was shoved from the back and my chest hit the door.

"How dare you?"

I spun around to face Sophie. The makeup under her

eyes was smeared, and I instantly hated myself for hurting her. It didn't matter that she hurt me too.

"You think you know everything, don't you?" She was right in my face, and the urge to kiss her even through my anger was overwhelming.

"I don't know shit, Sophie." I held my hands out wide. "That's the problem here, isn't it?"

Her small hands balled into fists. "Did you for one second think that maybe you should ask me? Did you consider that maybe you should have talked to me instead of my family?"

"For what?" I was as angry as she was. "You're leaving. Congratulations by the way. That's an amazing opportunity."

Her eyes narrowed farther. "You are such an asshole."

"You've known that for years, remember? Or did you suddenly forget about our past that you've hung over my head for as long as I can remember." I was baiting her. This I could handle. This fighting. I wanted her to fight, it was the walking away I couldn't take.

"I hate you." She barely whispered the words.

"No. You don't." I shook my head and reached out for her, but she took a step back.

"Just leave, Jase. Isn't that what you're good at?"

"There it is." I grinned at her. "And convenient timing considering."

I opened the car door, and this time she let me.

"I hope you have a great time in Seattle, Soph. Maybe you'll get lucky and have another boss you can fuck."

She jolted back as if I had slapped her, and I instantly regretted the words.

"Fuck you, Jase." She spit the words at me.

"Ah, darling. You already have."

I started to close the door, but her hand reached out and stopped it. "I turned down the job. So it looks like I lost our little bet, huh?"

My gaze snapped up to hers. "What?"

"Yeah. The wedding has barely even begun, and I've already gotten fucked." She laughed, a bit crazy. "Maybe if I fuck that boss from Seattle he'll let me change my mind."

"Sophie."

"No." She shook her head and let go of the door. "Fuck you."

Then she turned her back to me and did what I had been accusing her of the whole time. She walked away.

CHAPTER 25
JASE

I walked into the office with what felt like the biggest hangover of my life.

Sophie had refused to talk to me after our fight on Saturday. I had blown up her phone like a certified stalker, but she had ignored each and every one of my calls.

When I showed up at her apartment on Sunday with no answer, her momma told me that she wasn't there and to give it some time.

Time.

I didn't have time to give her.

For all I knew, she had already called Keller Architecture and Design and begged them to ignore her refusal of the position. I knew it was selfish of me, but I prayed that they didn't.

If she left for Seattle, I would never get her to forgive me. I needed her here. Even if she didn't forgive me, I didn't know if I could be that far away from her without going crazy.

The only thing I was certain about was that I was at Sophie's mercy.

Her decisions would affect the both of us. Whether she decided to leave or stay. Whether she decided she wanted to be with me or not.

It was all up to her.

When I walked into the office, Annie was already sitting at her desk which was a rarity. I was almost always here before anyone else.

Annie looked up and her smile instantly dropped from her face. "What's wrong?" She came around her desk as I tried to sneak past it.

"Nothing's wrong."

"Don't lie to me." She matched my pace and followed me to my office. "I can see it in your eyes."

I unlocked my door and huffed. "I'm fine, Annie. I swear."

"What can I do? Do you need coffee?"

I smiled at Annie's concern, but there was nothing she could do for me. Not now.

"Unless you can magically make Sophie appear." I plopped down in my chair. "Then there's nothing you can do."

Annie looked at me with a confused expression. "Do you want me to get her? She's in her office."

"She's here?" I shot back up out of my chair.

"Yes?" Annie said it like a question. "Is she not supposed to be?"

I pulled her into my arms and gave her a tight squeeze. "This is exactly where she's meant to be."

I left Annie standing in my office looking more confused than I had ever seen her, and I went straight to Sophie's office. Her door was slightly ajar as I walked up, and I quickly pushed it open, not caring who was inside.

The only thing that greeted me was an empty office.

I went in search of her and almost passed the break room when I heard her soft laugh. I pushed through the door as quickly as I could and found her leaning against the counter with a cup of coffee in her hand. She was talking to a few guys from our office, but I didn't give a shit about them.

"Sophie, I'm so sorry." The words were past my lips before she even looked up at me.

She smiled as she looked from me to our coworkers. "There's nothing to forgive, Mr. Hale."

"Drop the Mr. Hale shit."

She pushed off the counter and forced a smile to them. "I'll catch you all later."

They mumbled their goodbyes, but I didn't take my eyes off her. Her hair was piled in a messy bun on top of her head, and although she looked beautiful, it was impossible not to see the puffiness under her eyes.

She slid past me out the door, making sure not to touch me, and I immediately turned on my heel to follow her.

"I have work to do, Jase." She walked into her office, and I caught the door just as she tried to close it.

She didn't fight me as I pushed it open then closed it behind me. She just sat at her desk and looked up at me with a bored expression.

"What can I do for you?" She brought her coffee back to her lips.

God, she was so damn good at pissing me off. I came in here to apologize, and already, she was making my blood boil.

"Forgive me." I put my hands on the back of the chair

that sat in front of her desk, and her eyes snapped to them as I tried to hold my shit together with the force of my fingertips into the leather.

"I already told you. There's nothing to forgive."

I shook my head and tried to block out her words. "I thought you were leaving." She finally looked back up at me. "I didn't mean anything I said. I was just angry."

"We're good at that, huh?" She cocked her head to the side. "Making each other angry."

"No." I shook my head.

"Yes, Jase. That's what we do. This." She moved her hand back and forth between the two of us. "It's too much. Too complicated."

"That's bullshit."

"It's the truth." She said the words as if she believed them, but her eyes told differently. "It would never work."

"So, what? That's it. You decide we won't work, and you give up?"

She was getting angry now. Good. I would take her anger over her impassive attitude any day. "I'm not giving up. It's called being an adult, Jase."

"Fuck that." I started moving around her desk, and she tensed. "It's an excuse."

"So what if it is." She stood from her chair and stared at me. We were only a couple feet apart now, and I was dying to reach out and pull her into my arms. "I don't have to have a reason to not want to be with you."

I swallowed at her words and reminded myself that I hurt her. "No. You don't." I took a small step toward her, and she took a step back. "But you should know that I'm in love with you."

"Oh." She threw her hands up in the air. "You're all of a

sudden in love with me. That's supposed to make everything better."

"I'm not all of a sudden in love with you." I ran my fingers through my hair. "I've been falling in love with you for far too long."

"And you're just now telling me this?" She put her hands on her hips.

"It's not something you just blurt out." I threw up my hands in frustration. "You haven't told me yet either."

She shook her head over and over as she spoke. "I don't love you."

"Lie to yourself, sweetheart, but you fucking love me."

"No. I don't." Her eyes started to fill with tears, and I couldn't take it anymore.

I needed to hold her. I needed to feel her skin against mine.

I pulled her against me. She pressed her hands on my chest in a weak attempt to keep me away, but I felt the way her fingers ached to curl into my shirt and pull me toward her.

I lifted her chin with the pad of my finger and forced her to look up at me. "Please tell me you're staying."

"I shouldn't." She started shaking her head, but I gripped the sides of her head to stop her.

"I want you to."

"You don't always get what you want, Jase." She sounded more resigned than angry, and it killed me.

"I just want you."

Her eyes slammed shut as if she could force out my words.

"I shouldn't love you."

"But you do," I whispered against her jaw and felt her skin against my lips for the first time in what felt like forever.

She nodded her head and her fingers finally curled in my shirt.

I didn't give her a moment to second-guess it or take it back. I tightened my hands on her face, and I brought my lips to hers.

I couldn't hold myself back as I kissed her. I wanted to make up for all the time we had lost, every second that I should have had her in my arms.

She kissed me back just as desperately.

We were sliding lips and clashing teeth. She was frantic whimpers while I couldn't do anything other than breathe her in.

I fell into her chair with her still against me, and she quickly straddled me without once breaking our connection. Her hands fell to my belt, and she impatiently tugged it open while I bunched her skirt around her hips.

She pulled my cock out of my pants as she lifted onto her knees, and barely managed to get her panties pulled to the side before she brought herself back down on me.

We both groaned as I filled her to the hilt. I wrapped my arms around her back, holding her against me, and she buried her face in my neck as she rolled her hips against me.

We were so in sync, our bodies fighting each other in the same desperation, and I barely had to touch her before her pussy clamped down around me.

"I love you." I let my words linger against her skin as I thrust up into her and felt the tiny shocks of her body.

"I..." She threw her head back and started riding me harder. She was so fucking close. "I love you too."

I thrust up into her harder as I pulled her down onto me. Her thighs shook against mine, and it was only a moment later that her entire body tensed above me before she finally let go.

She cried out my name, and it was the final push I needed. I pulled her impossibly close and thrust up into her one last time as I followed her over the edge.

I was uncertain about most things in life, but this, this was exactly where I was meant to be.

Her head was against my racing heart, and I tried to slow my breathing as I rubbed my hand down her back.

"What now?" she whispered so quietly I barely heard her.

"We should probably stop fucking in the office."

A laugh bubbled out of her, and she smacked my arm.

"I don't think Mr. Norman had this in mind when he said he's fine with us dating."

She put her hand between us and pushed up enough to look at me. "So, this is it? We're dating now?"

She said it in a joking tone, but her eyes looked as nervous as I felt.

"If not." I tucked a piece of hair behind her ear. "I can't wait to see what happens when we start."

She laughed, and I could feel myself plummeting. And in that moment, I knew, whatever this was, the madness, the fire, the punch to the gut when I looked at her, I never wanted to go without it again.

EPILOGUE
SOPHIE

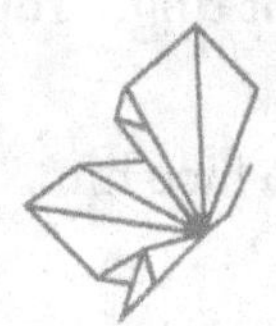

ONE AND A HALF YEARS LATER

I stood smack-dab in the middle of the construction site and looked around. It was crazy how quickly the buildings had started to go up after we finally got through all the red tape.

I was shocked when the team of the Anderson Development had chosen my plans. Shocked, scared, and a hell of a lot overwhelmed. If it hadn't been for Jase and, as much as I hated to admit it, Tom, I probably would have taken my plans and ran.

But Jase wouldn't let me.

He wrapped his arms around my middle and pulled me back into his chest. "What are you thinking about?"

I looked around at the crazy amount of work that was being done. "It's insane to think that I helped design this."

"Believe it, baby." He tightened his arms around me. "You looked super fucking hot doing it too."

I jabbed my elbow into his chest. "You're a pig."

"Yeah." He rubbed his nose along my neck. "But I'm your pig."

I snorted and felt his lips form into a smile against my skin.

"Pretty soon." He gripped my hand in his and rubbed his finger over my engagement ring. "You won't be able to get rid of me."

I turned in his arms to face him. "Have you ever heard of divorce?"

"Nope." He exaggerated the word.

"But I have heard that make-up sex with your wife is pretty amazing."

I rolled my eyes and wrapped my arms around his neck. "Well, you don't know how to act so we have plenty of make-up sex now."

"It'll be different once we're married." He grinned at me.

"Who told you that?"

"Your brother."

"Eww." I tried to push him off of me, but he wasn't having any of it.

"Just because he's your brother doesn't mean he doesn't have sex."

"But it does mean that you shouldn't be talking about our sex life with him."

"Technically, we were talking about his." He shrugged. "He acts just like you when I talk about our sex life."

"That's because my brother shouldn't know anything about my sex life."

"We tried that before, remember?" He smirked at me. "It got me a fist to the jaw."

"That was different." I rolled my eyes before looking

toward the team of workers who were packing up their trucks. Some music was playing from one of them, but I couldn't make out the song from where we stood.

Jase cupped his hand around his mouth. "Turn it up."

A couple of the men laughed, but one went to the driver side of his truck, and a moment later, the song rang out through the construction site.

Jase immediately started rapping to Missy Elliott, but I backed away from him with a laugh on my lips.

"Come on, babe. This is your jam." He thrust his hips in the air before swiveling them around in a circle.

"We are at work." I covered my mouth to hold in my laughter.

He moved a step closer to me. "It doesn't matter where you are when your jam comes on. It just takes over."

He gripped my hips in his hand and started rapping at the top of his lungs when I tried to pull away from him. The workers stopped what they were doing to watch us. Jase forced my hips to shake in his hands, and I didn't miss the catcall followed by an uproar of laughter.

I couldn't stop my laughter or the shake of my hips.

"Your men are going to think you're a prude," Jase said for only me to hear.

I smacked his arm, but he raised an eyebrow at me in challenge.

And he knew I couldn't back down from a challenge.

So, I pulled away from him, dressed in black slacks and a white button up blouse, and I shimmied my chest in his direction. The laughter around us raised to another level, and I grabbed my cellphone out of my back pocket and raised it to my mouth for a microphone.

Jase joined me as the two of us rapped for our audience

who was bent over in laughter. I shook my hips and did a little dance that I had seen on the internet but had no clue of the name.

The song ended, and Jase grabbed my hand and forced me into a bow. Everyone cheered and catcalled, and I could feel the blush crawl up my face. The men resumed what they were doing before our impromptu karaoke session, and Jase jerked my hand to pull me into him.

"You are so hot." He pressed his lips against mine.

"I remember once upon a time when you hated my rapping skills."

He shook his head. "Never."

"You're a liar." I shoved his shoulder.

He pulled me even tighter against him. "I'm not."

"So, what? You loved my rapping even back then?" I cocked an eyebrow at him.

"I loved everything about you."

I rolled my eyes. "You hated me."

"Yeah." He nodded his head with a grin on his face. "But fuck, I love you."

"I love you too." I laughed as he nuzzled his face into my neck. "Now take me home so I can have make-up sex with my fiancé."

"Are we fighting?" He leaned back to arch an eyebrow at me.

"I'm sure we can find something to fight about." I tugged on his hand and pulled him toward his car.

"Deal." He grinned at me, and my stomach tightened.

I would never get used to that grin aimed in my direction.

"You think you can piss me off before we get back to the house?"

He rubbed his thumb across his bottom lip, and I tracked its movement.

"I'll definitely give it a shot." He backed me up against the car door. "What about you?"

"I'll give it a double."

TROUBLE WITH THE FAKE BOYFRIEND

Keep reading for a sneak peek of Trouble with the Fake Boyfriend.

PROLOGUE
BROOKE

Why did weddings make you so damn emotional and/or horny?

Every wedding I had ever been to, I was either ready to fall in love with someone or I was ready to fall into bed with them. Neither one of those things was a good idea, but it didn't matter. No matter how much I pep talked myself before, those same damn feelings hit me like a ton of bricks every time.

And this time?

It was the worst idea possible.

Because for some damn reason, the only person I could see was the man standing across from me.

I was the maid of honor. He was the best man.

I was her best friend, and he was his.

And we lived right next door to each other.

Liam Gentry was gorgeous. Was it weird to call a man gorgeous? Probably, but I didn't care. There was no other way to describe him. Especially today when he was dressed like that. His hair was so dark it was almost black, but somehow still had a golden hue to it that seemed impossible, and it was always pushed back out of his face perfectly. The black suit he wore did nothing to deter me or my libido.

But none of that was what made my stomach tighten when he looked up from his feet to look at me.

It was that fucking smile.

It was perfect of course, everything on him was, but it was the way he used it as a weapon that fucked with my head.

He could turn it on and off without a second thought, and just as soon as you thought you were getting something real from him, he could slide that smile right back into place and make you think you imagined anything that came before it.

This was why I stayed away from Liam Gentry.

Men like him were trouble. I knew that firsthand, and I had no interest in getting my heart broken by him. Not that he ever would.

When Tucker and Liam first moved into the apartment next to us, I had to tell my vagina to calm down as soon as I saw him.

Surely you've heard of love at first sight, but this wasn't that. This was pure lust.

Nothing more and definitely nothing less.

But he shut that crap down before I could even put on my matching bra and panties and make a move.

He wasn't interested in getting involved with "a girl like me." Whatever the hell that meant. I didn't want to marry the guy. I just wanted to see what his penis felt like on my insides.

But maybe he was right.

Being friends with him seemed like a lot smarter decision.

But none of those rational thoughts were helping my irrational lust and the way this damn wedding seemed to push them all back as I stared over at him.

I looked out across the crowd as our best friends recited their vows to each other. Surely, there had to be someone else here that I could use to take the edge off with to get Liam out of my head.

Because it had been a while.

A good long while and that apparently was a huge mistake.

Colossal.

Because Liam never looked as good as he did today, and I was having to have a silent discussion with my vagina about how she couldn't have him.

I looked through Tucker's other friends. Jase was hot as hell. I knew from the moment I saw him that he would be hot, dirty sex, but I also knew the moment I saw Sophie look at him that he was completely off limits.

There was also Ryan, but I barely knew the guy. And even though I was self-aware enough to know how bad a decision it was to sleep with a guy I barely knew at my best friend's wedding, I was also aware that a guy I barely knew was a better decision than Liam.

Ryan was good looking. He was more than good looking actually. His blond hair hung in his face in a way that made your fingers itch to slowly push it back, and I had no doubt it was intentional. Ryan always had a killer tan and shit-eating grin, and I would bet good money that he was a stellar lay.

He looked fun, playful, and nothing like his friend that

stood beside him with a chip on his shoulder that he tried not to let anyone see.

Everyone started cheering around me, and I pulled my gaze away from Ryan to whistle for my best friends as they kissed. They were perfect for each other, and I couldn't have been happier for Kennedy.

I handed her bouquet to her as she grinned at me with the biggest smile I had ever seen on her face then she took off down the aisle with the man of her dreams.

I wrapped my arm in Jase's as he led me back down the aisle, but I made sure to smile over at Ryan before I did so.

He looked a little shocked by the flirt, but he smiled back.

The reception was a whirlwind of activity and being shoved in different directions by the wedding planner, and it wasn't until I finally got to take a deep breath at the bar and grab a glass of champagne that I finally got a moment alone with Ryan.

"Ryan, has anyone told you how handsome you look tonight?"

He looked up at me from his beer, and by the way he didn't answer immediately, I wasn't sure if he realized that I was talking to him.

"Other than Tucker's mom, nope." He chuckled, and the sound was endearing. How had I not noticed that before?

"Well, I'm here to tell you." I tipped my champagne flute in his direction. "That you clean up well."

He seemed a bit surprised at my words, and I couldn't say that I blamed him. Ryan and I had only spoken a handful of words to each other before, and they definitely didn't sound anything like the ones that just left my mouth.

"I would say the same to you." His eyes roamed down my

body and over my bridesmaid's dress that fit me like a second skin. "But you always look beautiful."

I ran my finger down the lapel of his suit, and he tracked the movement inch by inch.

"You're sweet."

He took a step closer to me, almost unnoticeably so, but I noticed.

Apparently, so did Liam.

"Weddings wear me out." He saddled up next to Ryan, and Ryan pulled his attention away from me to look at his friend. "Anyone up for a shot?"

He didn't wait for either of us to answer. Instead, he ordered three shots of tequila from the bartender and thanked him as he quickly poured the shots.

Liam handed the first shot to Ryan before turning to me with a shot in each hand. He held the shot out to me and our fingers grazed as the glass slipped from his hand and into mine.

And I hated that a simple touch from him could stir more inside of me than this whole little charade with Ryan.

"To friends." He raised his glass and touched it to mine causing a tiny bit to slosh over on my fingers. His eyes didn't leave mine as he threw the shot back and swallowed it as if it was water.

"Friends." Ryan chuckled softly, and I pulled my attention away from Liam long enough to smile at him before I threw back the liquor that burned my throat.

I set my empty shot glass down on the bar next to Liam just as a new song started playing through the speakers, and I gave Liam my back as I asked Ryan, "Do you want to dance? I feel like dancing!"

Ryan grinned and I could tell he wanted to look to Liam,

but I didn't give him the chance. I took his hand in mine and pulled him to the dance floor. Kennedy and Tucker were dancing with the biggest grins on their faces, and I wrapped my arms around Ryan's shoulders as we began to dance alongside them.

Ryan gripped my hands in his and slowly unlaced my fingers before pushing me away from him and twisting me into a spin. My body hit his with a thud, and I couldn't stop laughing.

"These other boys don't have a thing on me." He wiggled his eyebrows, and I laughed some more as he dipped me.

"Boys? Are you a boy, Ryan?"

"You know what I meant." He rolled his eyes. "I'm a man."

"Don't start beating on your chest now. You're the one who said it."

I wrapped my arms back around his shoulders, and I felt so relaxed with him.

"I have several references that could attest to just how manly I am."

He was still grinning, and I swear it was the easiest damn grin ever, like nothing or no one could make it fall from his face.

"Oh yeah?" I looked around the room. "Are any of those references in this room? Should I start questioning the girls that line up to catch the bouquet, or is this more of a Mrs. Robinson situation?"

"I don't kiss and tell, Brooke. That wouldn't be very gentlemanly of me."

I cocked my head to the side and looked at him. "Good to know."

His smile widened, but his eyes didn't stay on mine for long. Instead, he looked to the bar before looking back at me.

"So what's the deal with you and Liam?" He looked uncomfortable as the words passed his lips.

"There is no deal." I shrugged my shoulders as we continued to dance.

"You sure?" He looked like he didn't believe me.

"I'm absolutely positive." Why the hell were we still talking about Liam. I was trying to get laid here and Liam was a buzzkill.

"Does Liam know that?" He nodded his head toward the bar, and I looked over my shoulder to follow his gaze. "Because it looks like one of my best friends is currently planning my death while we dance."

He was right. Liam was staring daggers at the two of us, and I wasn't sure if he realized it or not, but he was doing absolutely nothing to hide it.

"I don't know what his problem is, but I can assure you that it has absolutely nothing to do with me." I turned back to Ryan and tried to avoid the fact that I could still feel Liam's eyes on me.

Ryan lifted his fingers and tucked a stray piece of hair off my face. "I'd be willing to bet my left nut that it does."

"Only your left?" I moved my body closer to his and ran my fingers through the hair that hung in his forehead. It fell perfectly right back into place.

"Well, I'm pretty attached to both, but I need to at least reserve one for baby making. Could you imagine a world where there wasn't more of this running around?" He motioned to his face, and I had to bite my lip to stop myself from laughing.

"It would be tragic."

"Exactly, and I'm pretty sure Liam's planning to detach both from my body, so." He quickly looked to his left just as Liam stepped up to us. "Hey, bud."

Liam nodded his head in Ryan's direction but didn't return his easy banter. "Can I cut in?" He was staring straight at me.

Ryan started to pull away from me, but I latched on tighter.

"Ryan was actually just telling me his plans for making babies, and I have to tell you, it's a fascinating story."

"That's not exactly true," Ryan started to interrupt me, but I kept talking.

"I'd really like to learn more about it. Raincheck?"

Ryan turned his head away from me and Liam, and I didn't miss the way his body shook with silent laughter. Liam definitely wasn't laughing though. He was just standing there like an asshole staring me down like I was somehow ruining his night.

"Ryan?" Liam said his name through clenched teeth.

"Yeah?"

"I'd suggest you find someone else to make babies with tonight 'cause this isn't fucking happening."

"Who the hell do you think you are?" I narrowed my eyes at him and gripped the back of Ryan's shirt in my fists.

"I asked you to dance." He completely ignored my question and that just served to piss me off more.

"And I said fuck off."

Ryan looked like he wanted to be anywhere but there in the middle of the two of us, but I wasn't about to let him go.

"Brooke." Liam growled my name, but I didn't care. He could take the scowl on his face and his clenched fists and shove them right up his ass. I showed a little interest in someone else and all of the sudden he gave a shit. I didn't think so.

"Liam, is there something you need?" I turned to face him more, but I left my hands on Ryan. "Your friend," I made sure to enunciate the word as I pointed to myself, "is busy flirting with your other friend," I pointed to Ryan, "with the hope of getting laid at this wedding."

"Shit." Ryan said the word under his breath with a soft chuckle.

He stared at me, long and hard, and there was something about his anger toward me that was a bigger aphrodisiac than a wedding could ever dream of being. I rubbed my thighs together to ease the ache that had begun to build there and Liam noticed.

He reached out, wrapping his hand around my upper arm, practically engulfing it, as he leaned toward me. Ryan was still standing in front of me, but Liam didn't care.

His mouth was next to my ear and his words were strained as they caressed my skin. "You and I both know Ryan isn't the one you want to fuck. You either dance with me or I'll deck Ryan and carry your ass off this dance floor."

I turned toward him, our lips only centimeters apart. "You wouldn't dare."

"Test me, sweetheart."

I had no idea what his damn problem was. Was he the official cock block of this wedding or was he just going out of his way to cock block me? Either way, there was no way I was causing a scene at Kennedy's wedding, and with the way Liam was looking at me, I didn't doubt that he would hold true to his word.

"Ryan, I'm going to dance with your boy here, but don't go too far."

Ryan softly laughed as I let my hands fall from him, and I hated how entertaining this whole interaction was for him. "Good luck."

Once Ryan had his back turned, I stormed past Liam, but he grabbed my hand and pulled me to a stop before I could get too far. He pulled me toward him, my chest slamming into his, before he wrapped his arms around my waist and started to move.

I didn't so much as sway my hips.

"What, you can dance with him but you're too good to dance with me?" He was staring down at me, and I was doing everything in my power to avoid his eyes.

"Ryan wasn't an asshole to me. So, yeah."

"I wasn't trying to be an asshole." He sounded sincere, but I didn't care.

"It just comes naturally."

He smiled, that damn smile that I loved and hated, and for the first time since I knew Liam, I wanted to slap that look right off his face.

"Just dance with me, B."

I used to like when he called me that, but tonight it just pissed me off. "Don't call me that. What? Is it too much effort to use my full name?"

His smile got wider and he pushed his thigh against mine to force me to move on the dance floor. "It doesn't stand for Brooke."

Wait, what? "Then what does it stand for?"

"It's not important."

"The hell it isn't."

He wasn't listening to me though. He was lifting my arms and laying them against his chest. I watched as his fingers traced their way back down my skin, and I couldn't remember for a second why I was mad at him when his fingers skimmed over the delicate area just inside my elbow.

My fingers clenched, gripping his shirt, just as one of his hands skated around my body and pressed against the small of my back, forcing my hips against his.

His body began to move, and I had no choice but to move with him or I would have been left a hot mess in the middle of the dance floor. Not that I already wasn't.

It was another reason that Liam was a horrible idea. He made me flustered and irritated, and I didn't like being either of those things.

"Look at us." Liam was looking down at our bodies that were pressed so tight they were practically connected. "We're dancing."

"I'm technically being forced." I scoffed at how easily he could go from being a complete asshole to this. Whatever the hell this was.

"You don't look like you're being forced." He looked around the room. "Everyone is looking over here at us, and they all see how pliable you look in my hands. They all see how easy it was to convince your body to move with mine."

"I swear to God, Liam. You could make an art out of being an asshole."

"Thank you." His grin widened, and I watched his lips like I was somehow glued to their movement.

"It wasn't a compliment."

"You know I'm right." He turned us. His body moving mine with no difficulty.

"And what did they see when they watched me and Ryan dance?" I felt his body stiffen against mine as the words left my mouth. I probably should have regretted saying it, but I didn't. Getting a rise out of him made me feel powerful when I typically felt anything but around him.

"They saw what I did. How uncomfortable you were in his arms."

"I don't know about that." I picked at a small speck of lint off his shoulder. "I actually felt pretty comfortable there, relaxed. Ryan's funny. I bet he'd be fun in bed."

"Is that what you need?" He growled the words low for only me to hear. "To be fucked by someone at this wedding."

This is what I didn't understand. Men. I don't want you but no one else can have you. If I didn't want a guy, he could literally go screw anyone he wanted. I wasn't territorial over things that didn't belong to me.

"It would be a nice perk. I'd hate to waste all that waxing I had to do for this dress on nothing."

His jaw clenched and in a moment of insanity, I reached up and ran my thumb across the sharp edge.

"Ryan seemed like he would have been down for it if you hadn't interrupted us."

"Oh, I bet he would have." He looked out over the crowd as if he was searching for Ryan just to stare him down with all that aggression that was rolling off him.

"You're not the only one who has needs, you know? This little hand of mine" —I drummed my fingers down his neck — "can only do so much."

He snatched my hand in his, catching me off guard, and he stared down at me with a look that said he wanted to kill me. Good. We felt the same.

"I bet this little hand." He lifted my hand to his face and pressed a kiss to the inside of my wrist. "Could do so many things."

I didn't know if it was the kiss, his words, or the way he

spoke them, but my stomach tightened and I couldn't think of anything to say to him in return.

He pressed my hand back against his chest and kept it covered with his as he leaned down and spoke in my ear. "Is that what you need, B? You need me to fuck you and show you exactly what your hands could do?"

God, what was he saying?

Did I want him to fuck me? Um, one-way ticket to pound town for one, please.

But I didn't want his pity or his teasing. If he thought I wasn't capable of getting laid on my own, he had another thing coming.

"I'm sure Ryan could show me." His body stiffened again, and this time I thought he was going to walk away from me. Good. I needed him to walk away and give me a moment to clear my damn head.

But he didn't.

Instead, he gripped my hand in his and led me from the dance floor. I had no idea where he was taking me, and I could barely think, let alone keep up as he took angry steps in the opposite direction of where all the wedding activities were taking place.

"Where are we going?" I called out to him, but he didn't stop. Hell, he didn't even slow down.

He pulled me toward the house, and I swear my chest tightened so hard that I felt like I couldn't breathe. Joking around with Liam was one thing because he had drawn the line in the sand pretty damn clearly. But this? I had no freaking clue what to do with this.

We made it as far as the shadows before Liam pushed me against the house and stared down at me with a heavy breath. He searched my eyes, looking for what, I couldn't be sure. Permission? He had it. Want? It should have been clear as fucking day.

He lifted his hand, and I watched as it made its way toward my face. I expected him to gently touch me or hell, I don't know, pull me into a kiss. But he did neither. His thumb drug across my bottom lip roughly, as if he couldn't take another second of not touching it, as he watched.

"You sure about this, B?"

I nodded my head, the back of it still pressed against the house. I wasn't really sure what I was agreeing to, but I was agreeing anyway.

Liam ran his thumb back down my lip before he lifted my chin with the remainder of his fingers. He was staring down at me, and I couldn't even attempt to read him but suddenly I didn't care. Whatever his reasoning was for tonight, I would deal with the consequences later. I wanted him, badly, and there was nothing but him that could stop this.

He gripped my dress in his hand just above my hip, and I could practically feel the tension rolling off of him from that one small touch alone.

I sucked in a shallow breath as he moved his mouth closer to mine, his grip on my jaw tightening, my grip on reality floating away.

Then his lips pressed against mine gently, in complete contrast to everywhere else he was touching me, and I had to stop myself from begging him for more. When he didn't move, I slipped my tongue from my mouth and licked along the seam of his lips.

It was enough to unhinge him.

His mouth smashed against mine, his hand moved into my hair, and any chance I had of not letting the two of us cross this line went straight out the window. His lips moved against mine, and it took practically no effort on his part to force my lips apart. It was as if my body knew exactly what he wanted, and me and her? We were going to hand it over to him willingly.

I pressed my hips against his, begging for more of him, just as his tongue slid against mine, and I could feel how badly he wanted me. That simple reassurance fueled me. I lifted my hands from his chest, and for the first time since I had met Liam, I let my fingers skim over his skin freely.

I ran them along the edge of his sharp jaw. I dug them into his scalp as he nipped my bottom lip, and I used them to grip his hair and force him closer to me even though neither of us barely had room to breathe.

Breathing wasn't important in that moment though. Not when I was with him.

His hand crawled down my side leaving a trail of goose bumps before he roughly grabbed my hip, and I couldn't stop the soft whimper that left my lips.

"This is a bad idea." He said the words, but he didn't stop. My dress was slipping up my legs as he tightened his hand around the fabric and his mouth was moving along my jaw before he pressed his lips just below my ear.

"I've always had a thing for bad ideas." I was breathless as his teeth drug across my neck.

He kissed along my collarbone, making sure to take the time to run his tongue along the slight dip there, before he continued his way down my chest. He slipped my strap from my shoulder, and deep down I knew I should have been concerned about someone walking around the corner and finding us, but I wasn't.

My nipple pebbled as it met the evening air, and he

leaned back to look as he gently caressed it with his thumb and made me want to come out of my skin. I watched his every move as I attempted to calm my breathing, but then he looked up at me and held my eyes as he lowered his mouth.

The feel of his tongue against my skin had me squirming against him, the feel of his hand practically bruising my hip as he tried to hold in both his restraint and mine had me forcing my hips harder into his. Liam Gentry was a tease. He had been since the moment I met him, and I wasn't sure if I could handle another damn moment of it.

I reached forward, my hand skimming over his groin, and his mouth on my nipple was no longer soft or playful. He reached up, dropping the other strap and my dress fell, the fabric bunching just below my ribs.

"God." He took a small step back to look at me, my breasts completely on display, my shoulders pressed against the house, my hips still searching for his. "You are so damn beautiful."

I smiled at him, but I didn't need his words or admiration. I had been called beautiful by so many men during sex that I was beginning to feel lazy at this point, but I knew that's what they wanted me for. My beauty. My body.

And even if my chest did ache a little at the thought when it came to Liam, I had become used to the idea a long time ago.

He ran his hand from just below my jaw to the center of my chest, and I took that slow, calculated moment to try to clear my head and lock any possible feelings into the vault where they belonged.

His hand stopped right at my ribs, where it tightened before he used it to lift me off the wall and spin me as if I weighed nothing at all. His chest against my bare back, he pushed the stray hairs off my neck before pressing a soft kiss in their place.

He wrapped my hands in his, his practically engulfing mine, before he lifted them and pressed them against the house. The move forced my back to arch, and he only intensified the movement when he lifted my dress above my hips and pulled them further back against him.

I spread my feet apart, giving myself better stability, and I almost died as I stood there in that position waiting for him to touch me.

He ran his hand over my ass, taking his time to trace every curve, and by the time he finally reached the seam of my thighs, I was practically panting. His fingers touched the edge of my panties, and I jolted forward, not quite ready for his touch while simultaneously begging for it.

"How wet are you?" he said into my ear, his body pressing into me, as he teased me along my panties. "Do I need to eat this pussy before I fuck you or are you already ready for me?"

I shook my head, but I didn't know why. What was I saying? No, I didn't need him to put his mouth on me because I was already dripping wet for him, or no, I couldn't live another moment until he did?

His hand finally slipped under the thin fabric of my thong, and my soft moan met his the moment his skin touched mine.

"So fucking wet." He slid his finger over my clit, spreading the moisture as he went before his hand slid out of my panties and I felt like I was going to die.

I felt him shift behind me, and I took a deep breath as I waited for him to slide inside me. But just as my panties slipped to the side, I felt his tongue against my pussy from behind and my hands almost fell from the wall.

If anyone found us right now, there would be no denying what we were doing. There would be no getting out of it, but I didn't want to get out of anything. I never wanted to get out of the way Liam was making my body feel or the way his tongue was moving against my skin like he was starving and I was the only thing that could satisfy his hunger.

"Oh God." I dropped my elbows to the house and pressed my forehead against the cool exterior as I tried to focus on holding myself upright just as his teeth grazed my clit. "Liam." I didn't know why I was saying his name. I didn't want him to stop, but I also knew this entire damn wedding was about to hear me scream if he didn't.

He didn't care though.

He gripped my shaking thighs in his hands and continued to lick me without abandon.

I pressed my mouth against my forearm, and I used my own skin to muffle my cries as my orgasm stormed through my body and my knees began to give out below me.

I didn't need to worry though. Liam caught me, moving his body behind mine, his arm around my waist.

I had barely caught my breath, but I didn't care. I wanted him. All of him. Every bit that he was willing to give.

If his hurried touches and rushed breaths were any indication, he wanted me too.

And there was nothing that made me feel more powerful.

I spun toward him, my shoulders still pressing against the house, and I lifted my dress just above my hips as he watched, entranced. For a moment, I thought he was going to do nothing but stare at me, and I was sure I was a sight. I could feel the flush on my chest and my face from what he had just done to me, and I knew he could see the wild want in my eyes. There was no chance of me hiding it.

He leaned forward, his mouth possessing mine, and even though it wasn't a thought that I wanted to have, I knew that I had never been kissed like this before.

I worked his belt buckle as fast as I could, desperate to get more from him, and the way his fingers were rushing over my skin proved him to be just as eager.

It was the moment I had been waiting for since I first laid eyes on him. I was finally going to fuck Liam out of my system, scratch that itch that had seemed to take over my every thought.

My hand slipped under his slacks, and he breathed my name in a way that made my toes curl as my hand tightened around him.

He started to say something, a plea, begging me to stop, or a declaration of love, I wasn't sure. Because I never got to hear it.

Instead, Liam jerked my hand from his pants like I was burning him. I didn't understand what was happening until Liam forced my dress back down my hips and I heard voices coming around the corner of the house.

Voices that were too close.

Liam took a step back from me, a step that put so much distance between us I could feel the absence of him before he ever moved. I pulled up the top of my dress up just as he spoke.

"What's up, man?" Liam nodded to a guy I had never seen before as he rounded the corner.

They clapped hands and patted each other on the back

all while I stood there with my back against the wall and my heart in my throat.

"I have to head out." The guy's eyes landed on me before he looked back at Liam with a smile on his face. "You enjoy yourself though."

Liam ran his hand over the back of his head, and I swear I had never seen him look so uncomfortable. His friend didn't seem to notice, but I did. I always did.

"Yeah." Liam chuckled but didn't even acknowledge my existence. I was just the girl that he left high and dry, well definitely not dry, like I was nothing more than an easy fuck, and I guess I wasn't. "I'll catch you later."

It took a moment after he walked off before Liam turned back toward me, and I knew before I even saw his face the moment we were having was gone.

If I couldn't still feel the touch of his hands on my skin, I would have thought that I dreamed the whole thing.

He regretted this.

"This was a mistake." He took a step toward me, and I wished I could step back. I wished I could get as far away from him as possible in that moment.

I nodded my head, because he was right. Liam Gentry was a fucking mistake, and I was an idiot for ever thinking differently.

DIDN'T GET ENOUGH?

**You've fallen for the trouble.
Now it's time to meet the cowboys who'll ruin
you for anyone else.**

If you like your romance dirty-mouthed, slow-burn, high heat, and downright addictive, you'll want to head straight to the Calloway Ranch.

Keep Reading for a sneak peek of
Cowboy Casual!

CHAPTER 1
BLAIRE

The photos landed in my inbox at 5:37 p.m. Another email, this one with the subject line URGENT: For Review- Grant Chandler Jr.

I barely blinked. Just another Thursday at Senator Monroe's office, where my job as press assistant meant I spent half my time putting out fires before they spread all over the internet. A few clicks, some carefully crafted lies, and by dinner, the world would be slightly less on fire and my father's re-election chances marginally more secure.

I spent four years at Duke getting my marketing degree, and here I was, a glorified janitor for my father's indiscretions and political messes. My professors would be proud to see that their star pupil's primary skill set had become making scandals disappear before they hit the trending page.

But the name at the top of the email wasn't my father's. It was my fiancé's.

The Chandlers had been bankrolling my father's campaigns since before I came to live with him, their hedge fund fortune buying the influence that kept both families comfortable. Four years ago, my father seated me next to Grant at a fundraiser. I was finishing my last year at Duke, and my father's eyes gleamed with approval every time Grant leaned in to whisper something that made me laugh.

Two hours and three glasses of merlot later, I'd mistaken his calculated attention for charm, and the next morning, roses crowded my tiny apartment doorway with a note that simply read, "Dinner? -Grant."

That one yes led to a diamond ring that had been on my finger for the last fourteen months, and now the wedding was a little over a hundred days away.

I opened the email, and the images loaded one by one. I noticed Grant first, then his assistant, who was splayed across his mahogany desk. Her blouse was unbuttoned, and his fingers tangled in her dark hair while the other hand gripped her skirt, wrinkling the expensive fabric I'd complemented her on last month. There was a hunger in his eyes I'd never seen in our bedroom.

More images followed as I scrolled, each one a blow. My stomach clenched. There they were in a D.C. hotel elevator, and the timestamp mocked me. Taken exactly fifteen days after the engagement party my father had thrown for us. Another showed them at some dimly lit bar. Grant wore a navy suit with a pale blue tie I'd tied for him the morning of his keynote speech. She draped her thigh across him, and his hand disappeared beneath the hem of her dress.

I scrolled through the evidence of his betrayal. In some, they were alone. In others, they exchanged secretive touches at campaign events where I stood just yards away, smiling for donors while his fingers found her waist.

The first photo was from thirteen months ago, and the most recent was from yesterday afternoon.

My vision blurred as I stared at the photos. A laugh from the bullpen made me flinch, and my gaze landed on the framed picture on my desk. Grant and I were at the Children's Hospital benefit. Grant's hand gripped my hip, his fingers digging in enough to remind me to stand straighter for the cameras. I'd wanted to wear the black dress I'd picked out myself, but he'd replaced it with the lavender gown that was hanging in our closet when I returned from work. "Trust me," he'd said, his voice firm.

I waited for the rage, for the tears, but found neither. Instead, my fingers shook against the keyboard as the room tilted and narrowed around me. In that moment, I felt the snap of that invisible thread that bound me to this life, to my father's ambitions and Grant's possessive hands.

In its absence came the rush, the flood, the name I'd locked away years ago.

Colt.

I physically recoiled from my own thoughts. *No. Not now. Not him.* I'd buried him beneath years of careful compartmentalization, sealed him away in the darkest corner of my heart where dangerous things belonged. He'd gutted me in ways Grant's betrayal couldn't touch, yet here he was, the first name my mind reached for.

The contradiction made me sick. Hating him and the physical ache of wanting him after all these years. I feared what that meant about who I really was beneath all these perfect, polished lies I'd wrapped around myself like expensive armor that suddenly felt paper thin.

I stood so fast my chair clipped the wall and made the edges of my vision pulse. There was a ringing in my ears as I willed myself not to look at the humiliating photos again. Everyone in this office would see them soon enough, and I should have been doing damage control. That was my job, but I suddenly couldn't give a shit about this job.

Instead, I walked straight out into the hall, closing my office door behind me with a soft click. My heels echoed on the tile as I moved, mechanical and purposeful, each step meant to keep the panic from overtaking me.

The hallway outside my office was lined with campaign posters, and today the images of my father felt like sentries watching me, silent and expectant. I tried to draw a full breath, but the air stuck in my throat and went nowhere.

I picked up my pace, crossing the bullpen and weaving past the clutch of interns hunched over their laptops. Someone tried to get my attention, but I brushed past, offering only a brittle smile I hoped passed for apologetic. The elevator was slow as hell, so I ducked into the stairwell, grateful for the emptiness and the way the steps forced my body to move.

Three flights down, I stopped, leaning against the cool cement wall. My phone buzzed in my pocket, and I yanked it out, half expecting a message from Grant. But it was my father's assistant's name looking back at me.

Judy: Senator Monroe would like for you to meet him in his office immediately.

I stared down at the screen as if my entire future hadn't just imploded.

I should have been thinking about Grant. His betrayal. The years I'd spent smoothing his rough edges, convincing myself we were in love instead of two people playing assigned roles in someone else's strategy. I should have been furious or at least humiliated. But standing in that cold stairwell, an emptiness clawed through my chest, a ravenous, familiar void that didn't belong to Grant at all.

The realization ached inside me like a bruise pressed too hard, spreading from my sternum outward until even my fingertips felt tender with the truth I'd spent years denying. My body remembered what my brain had worked overtime to forget. His thumb tracing the freckles across my collarbone, the lake water dripping from his eyelashes as he surfaced beside me, the way my name sounded like a prayer when he whispered it against my neck at dawn. I hated how easily these memories returned, how they still burned beneath my skin while Grant's betrayal felt like nothing more than a paper cut.

I despised myself for it, for looking at evidence of my fiancé's infidelity and feeling only relief tangled with shame. The pain of losing Colt had carved hollows inside me I'd filled with pretty lies and my father's approval.

I started to turn back toward my father's office, because that's what the text demanded and that's what a dutiful daughter would do. But my body revolted. My hand hovered above the banister, knuckles white against the chipped paint, and I looked up the stairwell, concrete spiraling overhead.

Then my gaze dropped, my ears ringing, and saw an exit sign pulsing red at the base of the stairs like a dare. I pressed downward, footsteps echoing against the steps, and the farther I got from the office, the easier it was to breathe. My body was moving faster than my thoughts, and that felt like freedom.

By the time I hit the last step, my legs were numb. I didn't hesitate at the landing, didn't even process what I'd do next. Instead, I barreled toward the side exit, shoved open the steel door, and found myself in the narrow alley between the Monroe Senate offices and the looming black glass of Chandler & Chandler.

The sun hung low between the tall buildings, gilding the edges of everything it touched and forcing me to shield my eyes. When the door slammed behind me, I tried to breathe as my reflection fractured across the dark, mirrored windows of Grant's building. Three days ago, I'd walked through those same doors with his favorite sandwich and a smile, playing the role of the doting fiancée for an audience of receptionists.

I should've stopped to think and called my father. I should've done what I'd been trained to do. But all I could see was Grant's hand on another woman's thigh, and the way his smile had always held a flicker of calculation. For four years, I'd filed myself down, smoothed away any parts of me that might snag on propriety or expectation. Now something untamed and forgotten stirred beneath my ribs, screaming for me to be reckless, even as my father's voice in my head listed all the ways this would destroy everything I'd worked for.

I could feel myself being torn between the wild-hearted girl my mom had raised me to be and the dull woman my father had created.

Grant's building was emptying for the evening. Men and women in tailored suits filtered out the revolving doors, but I didn't slow down. I ignored the polite smiles offered by familiar faces. A few gazes caught on me, lingering a bit too long, and my skin prickled beneath their stares. The knowing glances made my stomach twist. Had they all seen the photos already? Or worse, had they watched Grant and his assistant slip in and out of his office for months while I'd been the oblivious fiancée?

I flattened my shaking hands against my skirt, smoothing wrinkles that had set in like permanent creases. My cheeks burned with each heartbeat, a flush I couldn't hide, but I lifted my chin and locked my shoulders back, marching into Grant's building before I could stop myself.

I passed the security desk, and the guard's eyes flicked up, then away. No need to check my ID when my father's face was on billboards and my fiancé's name was etched on the side of the building. I crossed to the elevator bank and jabbed my finger against the executive floor button, leaving a smudge on the polished brass.

The ride up was dizzying. Every surface in the elevator was a mirror, and three different women were reflected back at me. There was the Senator's daughter in her expensive suit and perfect posture purchased with years of correction. Then the jilted fiancé, with anger burning behind her trembling chin and firmly pressed lips where she'd learned to swallow her voice.

And then there was *her*. The one with wide eyes and color high in her cheeks, the one who looked like my mother. I wanted to scream at her, beg her to run, to fight, to do anything.

I'd let them kill her so slowly I hadn't even noticed she was dying.

The elevator groaned somewhere above me, the floor indicator ticking up, and I caught my mother's eyes in my reflection. Her dare and mischief flickered there, then disappeared beneath my father's careful mask. I touched my face, half-expecting to feel her sunlight warming my skin, but my fingers met only the sweat-damp foundation I'd applied that morning to cover my freckles.

My mother wouldn't recognize me if she saw me now, and I hated the way my mind still drifted to Colt, desperately wondering if he'd be the one person who could still see through to whatever remained of me.

What the hell was wrong with me? I should have been devastated about Grant, not feeling this treacherous relief.

The elevator jerked to a stop. I closed my eyes for a single, shaky breath, then wiped away a stray tear before it could mar my mascara. Just one tear was all I allowed myself to shed for the girl I used to be, the girl who'd been taught her worth came from men who never really loved her.

A soft chime announced my arrival as the doors parted to reveal a wall of windows framing the sunset-washed skyline. The remaining staff sat at their desks, sliding papers into briefcases and shutting down computers, their gazes carefully avoiding mine as I moved toward the frosted glass door that separated me from Grant's office.

Without knocking, I shoved open the door, and they sprang away from each other. His assistant met my gaze while her fingers straightened her shirt. Mascara tracks stained her cheeks.

Grant ran his fingers over his tie and offered his practiced smile. "Blaire, baby. What are you doing here?"

His assistant turned away, busying herself with paperwork on his desk, but I caught the way her hands shook.

I almost felt sorry for her.

"I thought we were meeting for dinner?" Grant's voice overlapped itself, the end of the sentence scraping against the beginning, like he was trying to race ahead of the silence

I'd brought into the room. He took a step around her, positioning himself directly in front of me.

"Don't act like you don't know that I've seen the photos." My voice was steady, but my hands trembled so hard I had to dig my nails into my palms to hold them still. "How long has this been going on?"

There was a twitch in his jaw, but he kept his mask perfectly in place. "Come on, don't do this here." He tried to close the space between us, palm open, but I jerked away so fast I nearly toppled a crystal award he'd won for service to his community off his bookshelf.

"Do not make a scene," he hissed, jaw clenched tight, and eyes darting to the open door behind me.

The command landed like a slap, and my heartbeat thundered in my ears as that wild-hearted Blaire clawed her way out.

"Should I whisper about you fucking your assistant, Grant?" I didn't recognize my own voice, how it carried across the room. "Would that be more convenient for you?"

His eyes darkened as his shoulders squared. "We should discuss this at home. Privately."

He reached for my elbow, but I stepped back. "No."

"Blaire." He said my name like he was speaking to a trained dog, and I recoiled.

"Don't touch me," I said, and I heard the tremor in my voice, which only made me angrier, but the look on Grant's face told me the words landed as I intended. "Nothing you say will change what you did."

"Blaire," he tried again, gentler now. "Let's take some time to think about how we want to handle this, okay? I'll call your father—"

"Of course you will," I cut in. "You're such a fucking coward, Grant."

He flinched. Not enough that anyone else would notice, but I'd spent four years learning the tells of Grant Chandler. The tic in his jaw, the flicker behind his eyes when his composure slipped. I recognized the look of a man cornered, and it thrilled and terrified me that I was the one who'd put him there.

"This is my office. People are watching," he hissed as he angled his body like he was going to shut the door. "Let's be smart about this."

"Smart," I repeated, and the laugh that escaped me was raw and humorless. "Where were your smarts when you were fucking her on your desk? Did you think no one would notice? Or did you think I wouldn't care?"

"I never meant for you to find out like this," he said calmly. "I was going to tell you. I— I needed the right time. You know how your father is. How important this is for all of us."

I could hardly breathe as I thought of my father's ambitions, my own perfectly curated life, and the unyielding gravity of "all of us." It made me want to scream.

"My father." The words clawed at my throat as my gaze fell to the ring on my finger, the weight of the diamond suddenly crushing every bone in my hand.

"Yes, your father, Blaire," he said, drawing out each word as if I were too stupid to keep up. He leaned in, dropping the mask of concern for something infinitely colder. "Don't act fucking daft. He'll get a handle on this, and we'll figure it out."

"There's nothing to figure out." I shook my head. "I can't do this."

"Where the fuck else would you go?" He laughed, and his words hit hard, harder than I'd braced for. "You live in my condo, Blaire. You work for your father, whose campaign is funded by mine. The life you live is because of me, so don't act like you're better than this."

I had grown used to Grant's cruel words, but somehow, they still sliced through me like a blade. He was right, wasn't he? My clothes hung in his closet, my career existed at my father's mercy, and even my engagement ring had been passed down through generations of Grant's family. But I had built this life too. I had sacrificed for it, shaped myself to fit in it.

The phone on his desk rang loudly, making me flinch. His assistant lunged for it, her voice a distant buzz until she thrust the receiver in my direction, her eyes wide with fear. "Ms. Monroe, it's your father."

My stomach dropped as I brushed past Grant, my fingers clumsy as they closed around the handset.

"Dad—"

"Come to my office. Now." His tone was so measured and so infuriatingly calm that rage flooded me, making my teeth clench so hard my jaw ached.

"No." The word ripped from my throat, and I shook my head even though he couldn't see me. "You don't get to ask me to swallow this. Not for you. Not for him."

"Don't be foolish, Blaire. Grant made a mistake. All men make mistakes." My father's voice slithered through the phone like poison. I locked eyes with Grant across the room, watching him watch me, and I felt like I was suffocating.

My fingers trembled against the ring, twisting it once, twice, before hesitating at the knuckle. The diamond caught the light, beautiful and cold. I yanked it off, wincing as it scraped my skin, then traced my finger over the pale indent left behind. I squeezed the metal in my palm until it bit into my flesh, drawing comfort from the pain.

"Go to hell, dad."

I hung up before I could hear my father's response, and the phone clattered into the cradle.

Grant's eyes darted between my face and the ring clenched in my fist. I thought he was about to plead, but instead, he said, "You're being childish."

I tried to move past him, but Grant moved faster. His hand shot out, catching my arm above the elbow. He held on like he thought he could will the moment backward, as if the world would reset if I stood still long enough.

The heat of his palm bled through my shirt, and I remembered every time he'd touched me gently for the camera, every time he'd squeezed my shoulder in public, always anchoring me to his side. I'd mistaken that pressure for security, but now it felt like a vise.

"You're not leaving until we talk about this." His voice dropped to a growl, low and ugly. He yanked me closer, pulling me off balance.

I twisted my arm, trying to pry him off, but his grip tightened, his thumb digging into the soft flesh inside my elbow.

"Grant," his assistant whispered his name from behind me, but he didn't acknowledge her.

"You're hurting me," I gasped, and this time, I wrenched free.

His face went slack with surprise, as if he couldn't believe I'd dare resist him.

"Never put your hands on me again," I said, my voice steadier than my heart, as the diamond's edge bit into my palm.

Ten years ago, on a night that still woke me up sweating, I'd stood in the gravel driveway of my grandmother's house and hurled Colt's necklace at his chest because I couldn't make him choose me.

But I couldn't bring myself to hurl this ring at Grant, couldn't bring myself to care enough. I opened my aching fist and let the ring fall to the ground, watching it bounce once before settling.

I thought he might grab for me again, but he just stared, mouth tight, as I stepped past him into the hall. I walked in a trance, the blood in my ears so loud I barely heard Grant call after me.

But his words chased me with a desperate, low chuckle. "You'll be back."

I forced myself to keep walking, and I didn't stop until I was jabbing my finger against the elevator button, then again, harder. I didn't want to think about what would happen if I didn't leave right now, if I let the old gravity pull me back toward the familiar controlling orbit of Grant, my father, and all the plans they'd fused around me like a glass cage.

The elevator doors finally slid open, and I stepped inside. Four years of my life stood behind me. Security, status, a future. I pressed my back against the wall and watched the doors close, avoiding looking at my reflection. My hands shook as I pulled out my phone and dialed my grandmother's number.

She answered on the third ring, her voice calm and steady as always. "Hello."

I opened my mouth, but nothing came out but a strangled sound somewhere between a gasp and a sob.

"Blaire?" Panic edged her voice, crackling through the connection. "What's wrong?"

"Can I come home?" The words tumbled out, raw and clumsy. I waited for the guilt, the flood of regret for throwing away everything I'd built, but all I felt was an overwhelming, dangerous relief that flooded through my chest like the first breath after nearly drowning.

"Always, baby." No questions, no hesitation.

I pressed the button for the ground floor. The elevator plunged downward, and with it came visions of Colt, the curve of his jaw, the calluses on his fingertips, the weight of judgment I'd find in his gaze. My lungs seized at the thought. I was going back to the place I'd fled a decade ago, back to where Colt Calloway's words had severed me from my roots, but now those same roots called me home.

The Calloway Ranch Series

Cowboy Casual
Available now!

Small Town Smokeshow
Coming May 12th, 2026
Preorder now!

JOIN US IN HOLLYWOOD!

Want first dibs on new releases, bonus scenes, exclusive giveaways, and behind-the-scenes updates?

Subscribe to my Newsletter!

Want to hang out where the real fun happens: early ARCs, spicy secrets, giveaways, and all the juicy gossip before anyone else?

Become a member of Hollywood!

ALSO BY HOLLY RENEE

The Calloway Ranch Series:

Cowboy Casual

Small Town Smokeshow

The Veiled Kingdom Series:

The Veiled Kingdom

The Hunted Heir

The Rivaled Crown

Stars and Shadows Series:

A Kingdom of Stars and Shadows

A Kingdom of Blood and Betrayal

A Kingdom of Venom and Vows

A Kingdom of Fire and Fate

The Good Girls Series:

Where Good Girls Go to Die

Where Bad Girls Go to Fall

Where Bad Boys are Ruined

The Boys of Clermont Bay Series:

The Touch of a Villain

The Fall of a God

The Taste of an Enemy

The Deceit of a Devil

The Seduction of Pretty Lies

The Temptation of Dirty Secrets

The Rock Bottom Series:

Trouble with the Guy Next Door

Trouble with the Hotshot Boss

Trouble with the Fake Boyfriend

The Wrong Prince Charming

ACKNOWLEDGMENTS

Thank you to all the readers that have been such an amazing support! I can never thank you enough.

As always, a huge thank you to my husband for supporting all my dreams. I think it's impossible for me to be any more in love with you than I am today. I love you.

Thank you to my entire team who I couldn't do this without!

ABOUT THE AUTHOR

Holly Renee is a USA Today bestselling author of romance that crackles with tension, swoons with heat, and leaves readers giddy with delicious banter. Whether she's whisking you off to a moon-drenched fantasy kingdom or a Tennessee ranch filled with heartbreak and horses, her stories are fast-paced, emotionally charged, and undeniably fun.

Born and raised in East Tennessee, Holly is a married mom of two, a lake enthusiast, a lifelong lover of pink, and hopelessly obsessed with the kind of love that makes you scream into your pillow.

Find her at www.authorhollyrenee.com.